Flynn's
BOARDING HOUSE

Thanksgiving Blessings

LISA ANDERSON MCCORD

https://quantumdiscovery.net/

ISBN
978-1-959314-82-0 (Paperback)
978-1-959314-83-7 (eBook)
978-1-959314-81-3 (Hardcover)

Dedication

This book is dedicated to my mother Kate Anderson—my mom, my best friend. You touched more people in your lifetime than you could have ever imagined. I love you.

Table of Contents

Acknowledgments

To my husband, Pat, for all his love and support and for being my knight in shining armor when all things could and did go wrong, I love you.

To my children Katy, Maggie, Sean, and Ian, whom, although, I drove crazy during this new endeavor love me still as I them.

To my sister Mary Jo, and brothers, Ralph, Tom and John, nowhere on earth could there be a tighter knit family than ours. I love you all so much.

To my best friend Linda, God knew what he did when he placed us kitty corner all those years ago. I know that I would never have found as special a friend as you left to my own resources.

To my good friend Cath, who had struggles this past year but, still gave much needed positive support.

To all those at Quantum Discovery, thank you for all of your hard work, patience, and kindness; it's been immeasurable.

Chapter 1

Josh

It was late in the afternoon. The sky looked as though it had been painted with purple streaks fading into red. The sun had begun to rest at its most western horizon and lazily fell below the forest's tree line. The air had turned cool, and the leaves under his feet were crisp and dry. Josh stopped and, taking everything in, breathed deep and continued to walk. November usually felt colder this time of year, but Josh didn't mind.

He wore a pair of jeans, a white, buttoned-down oxford shirt, a soft leather bomber jacket and a worn pair of brown suede loafers, *his favorite*. Comfort and relaxed described his style. During the late afternoon, the gloaming, Josh felt especially peaceful and calm.

This was always his favorite hour. Dinner hour is a quiet retiring moment when most people settled down in their homes and got ready to share a meal and converse about their day. For Josh, it was his time for prayer and reflection.

Today was no different. Only today, he walked as he prayed and reflected on a place to hang his hat in this small town for the short time he intended to call home.

Josh knew his task would take shape and present itself in a way that he ascertained to be least expected. As he strolled, he contemplated on how long it had been since he'd been there among people. He also realized that he'd never been in this part of the world. However, his father's creation was in trouble. The United States seemed as good a region as any to begin his work. So here he was in Munising, Michigan, sent to make some sense of it all, to see if there was faith or hope to be found.

Josh walked for about three blocks in Munising, population two-thousand, when he came upon a large, old brick house. Attached to the bricked in porch was a sign that told of a Room for Rent. *This looks promising*, he thought. He looked up, prayed a silent thank-you, and strode up the long front path and climbed the stairs.

Chapter 2

Flynn McNamee

After a few raps on the door, an average-looking, balding, middle-aged gentleman answered. He was wearing a light-blue cardigan sweater and asked, "May I help you?"

"Yes," Josh replied. "I'd like to talk with you about the room you have for rent."

"Oh, okay, please come in." Josh and the gentleman walked in through a small call box into the large foyer and introduced themselves to each other.

"My name is Josh, Josh Davidson," he exclaimed, stretching out his hand in a friendly manner.

"Mine is Flynn, Flynn McNamee," he replied as he grabbed hold of Josh's hand. As quickly as he grabbed, he let go. He stepped back, shook his head, and said, "Whoa, what was that?"

"What?" Josh asked. "Oh, I'm sorry"—he looked quizzically at his hand—"It's interesting, right?"

"Well, yes. I've never had that happen before."

"The feeling is a bit like all the happy times and good memories of your life rushing through at once.

"How do you do that?" Flynn questioned.

"I'm not really sure. My father had always told me that I have special gifts, and that is just one of them."

"That's some gift," Flynn responded, slowly rubbing his hands.

Do you mind if I ask you a few questions before I show you the room?" Flynn inquired.

Josh had smilingly agreed, nodded yes and said, "Shoot." Flynn took a deep breath and began with a paper and pen from the table to his right, clearing his throat.

"Are you from around here?"

Josh seriously responded, "No, I'm from out of town."

"Okay, where exactly?"

"Well, I'm originally from the Middle East, but recently, I've been visiting family in Italy."

"All right, what brings you to Munising, Michigan? Do you have relatives and friends here?"

"No, I've never been to the United States before. I've always had a curiosity about it, especially the snow, which is something I've wanted to experience my whole life. I did some research, and Michigan seems to be a good state to experience snow, is it not?"

"Well, one thing for sure, here in Munising, we definitely manage our fair share."

Josh's face lit up. "Wonderful," he exclaimed. "I can't wait."

"I'll get back to you on that after your first winter season here." Flynn rubbed his chin, looked at his list, and continued, "How long do you plan on staying?"

Josh thought and replied, "Well, I'd like to get a job in town, depending on that and if everything else works out, I really have no plans to move on just yet, so I guess my answer is indefinitely." Finally, Flynn queried Josh for his identification, visa, and social security card. Josh reached into his back pocket for his wallet and presented all three without hesitation. Flynn then wanted to know if Josh was interested in seeing the area that he intended on renting to him.

"I'd love to."

Flynn told him, "It's at the top of the stairs, second door to the right. Just follow me." Josh found himself exploring as he walked.

To his right, he saw a large living area with an attached enclosed porch, to the left a beautiful oak dining room and what appeared to be a kitchen galley. Straight ahead, the maple stairway ascended to a landing with an ideal size window that Flynn mentioned has a spectacular view of Lake Superior; however, at night, that was not visible, but during the day, it was a sight to behold. A sharp left takes you up four more steps. At the top of the stairs was another foyer with two rooms to the west and two rooms to the east with a full bath straight ahead. Flynn walked first and opened the last bedroom door adjacent to the bath. He held the door and let Josh walk in first.

Josh stepped in, took one look around, and smiled. The first thing he noticed was the beautiful built-in bookcases along the far wall. Then he crossed the room to the window seat that sat below the grand glass window. Looking out, he viewed a site so picture-perfect he was rendered speechless. He couldn't believe the blessings he had been guided to. He turned to Flynn and said, "This is awesome. I'll take it."

Flynn asked, "Don't you want to know how much I want for it?"

"Oh, I'm sorry how much?"

"Well, $400 a month and $400 in advance."

"That's just fine. Here's $400 for the advance and $400 for my first month's rent." Flynn smiled and watched as Josh took the money from his wallet and handed it to him counting it out at the same time. They walked out of the room, and Flynn led Josh to a chart next to the washroom with other boarders' names on it.

"This is a bathroom time chart," he said. You fill in your name where there is an opening, and that will be your schedule for showers and such. This way, there's no arguing and getting in each others way in the morning."

"Hey, that's a great idea!" Josh exclaimed. "I'll be sure to do that as soon as I get all of my possessions moved in."

Josh smiled at Flynn and asked when it would be convenient for him to bring his clothes, books, and his other personal items over to his new room. Flynn told him any time the next day was fine, and he added that if he needed a place that night since he paid already, he was welcome to stay.

Now, this pleased Josh and surprised Flynn because he knew that he didn't know Josh, and he always did background checks on his boarders, but Josh seemed different. He wasn't sure why. He simply felt safe and comfortable around him. Maybe it was his smile or it was the peaceful easy way about him. The one unusual conundrum was that very unusual handshake of his. He wasn't sure; he just knew deep down he could trust him.

Josh said he wanted to go get a bite to eat and asked Flynn if he could recommend a place.

Flynn, rubbing his chin snapped his fingers and said.

"I sure do. They have great food and fantastic service. It's real down to earth home cooking, and they've got the best apple pie in the county." As they walked back down the stairs Flynn explained.

"You go right out the front door here, cross the street, and turn left at the first corner you come to. After that you'll go about two blocks you'll see it right there on your left, Jenny's Diner.

"Thanks Flynn, I should be back within the hour if you're sure it's ok."

"Sure, sure it's no problem at all."

"Great" Josh said, as he went to shake Flynn's hand again.

This time, Flynn hesitantly took his hand in preparation for that electrifying feeling. Surprisingly, this time, he felt something different—a nice, warm, calming sort of sensation. It took his breath away for a second. When he looked up at Josh, Josh was smiling at him. Letting go was like a spell had been broken. Josh asked if he was all right. Flynn's breath caught, and he responded by nodding and smiling. He just couldn't find the right words. The feeling was unlike any he had ever had; it was *sensational.* Josh said he'd be back later and turned to leave.

"Before I forget. Here's the key. I live in the little house right behind this one. If you need anything, I'll be there." As they headed down the stairs, Flynn told Josh, "I'll see you in the morning."

When Josh left, Flynn set out to put fresh linens on his bed and some clean towels on his nightstand, all the while wondering what it was about this guy. *He is so likable. I realize I should be leery*, he thought. *I'm sure he's okay. It's just a gut feeling I know. Somehow, I can't help thinking this young gentleman is special.*

Chapter 3

Amber

Josh walked a couple of blocks to the town square and found the quant diner called Jenny's. It had a big front window with booths lined up alongside it inside. Further in, he noticed an old-fashioned soda fountain counter with leather stools. In the center of the dining room, the tables were covered with navy and white checked tablecloths. Josh ambled in, picked a booth next to the window, sat down, and began to look at their menu. The waitress soon caught his eye and went over to where he was seated to take his order.

She welcomed him, then introduced herself as Amber.

Afterward, she explained the dinner specials and asked him for his drink order. When she placed his drink in front of him, she asked if he was ready to order. Walking back to the kitchen, she thought to herself, *This is a nice guy. And his eyes, they are ant unbelievable warm, gentle brown. It was like he could see into my soul.* As Amber put his hot meal in front of him Josh smiled up at her;clapped, and rubbed his hands together.

"This looks delicious and I'm starving."

"Well then", Amber started as she began to leave.

"I'll leave you to enjoy your meal in peace."

"No, no Josh pointed to the other side of the booth. I'm new here and would love a little company. Flynn told me this was the place to eat and it looks like he knows what he's talking about." Amber looked around at the almost empty diner and cautiously stated

"I'm sorry I'm not allowed to sit during my shift; I can however, visit a little since we are slow at the moment. You said you know Flynn, oh sorry, Mr. McNamee?"

"Yes I'm going to be staying at his boarding house for a while."

"That's nice, how long will you be staying?"

"I'm not sure yet. At least long enough to see the snow. I've never witnessed it before this will be my first time." At that Amber burst into laughter, which was music to Josh's ears.

"Well you are definitely in the right town and region for that. They're already calling for a snow storm tomorrow."

"Really, I can't wait." Josh continued to enjoy his meal and found through their comfortable conversation that the diner was slow, and she was somehow drawn to him. Amber was a sweet nineteen-year-old girl working her way through college. Being the first in her family to have the privilege to attend, she was very excited to be going. She went to the local junior college near her home, and then she would head off to the university and get her degree in education. Her parents and grandparents couldn't be prouder.

Josh and Amber talked on and on. He asked her questions, and Amber easily answered. They became quick friends. After he finished his meal, he paid his bill, and he said good night and left promising her he'd see her again soon. Amber smiled back and waved good-bye.

⚬

For some peculiar reason, Amber felt a little lonely when Josh left. She had no idea what had come over her. She had never talked to a stranger like that before. She had given him so much information about herself. Suddenly, she felt a little self-conscious. As she wiped down the tables and straightened the chairs, she searched her brain. Had she said anything that could lead to a dangerous encounter of some kind? *Now, let's see, we talked about religion. Why did I do that? We also hit on my parents, grandparents, school, my future, my dreams, and my boyfriend. Everything was safe. I did talk about my whole life. Oh well,* she thought. She finished closing straightening the chairs and tables. She stepped outside, said good night to Joe, the cook, and locked the door. Just then, her dad pulled up in his truck. Amber took a deep breath, put a smile on her face, and turned to greet him.

Chapter 4

Moving In

Josh walked back to his room at the motel and packed some of the essentials he would need and paid his bill. He explained that he'd be back in the morning for the rest of his belongings. The desk receptionist smiled and said that would not be a problem and thanked him for staying with them.

As he walked the few blocks to Flynn's he reflected on the conversations he had with Flynn and with Amber. After several moments, he realized that his father's reasons will be revealed soon enough. Knowing this and holding onto his faith was all he needed. For now, he was tired, and he needed to get some sleep.

He soon reached Flynn's humble home, climbed the stairs, and unlocked and opened the door. He took a note that was taped to the window. With a smile, he read:

> Please lock up behind you. I've gone to
> bed, Flynn.

Josh stepped across the threshold and glanced around the quiet house. In four easy strides, Josh was across the foyer and ascended the stairs to his room.

Once in his room, he saw the fresh linens that Flynn had laid out for him along with some clean towels placed neatly on the nightstand. On the pillow was a notation:

> Josh, breakfast is served at 6:30 and ends at 8:30 during the week and at 7:00 to 9:00 on Saturdays. Sundays, we have brunch beginning at 11:00 until 1:00 p.m."

Josh folded the note and set it on the nightstand. Then he grabbed his soap and towels went to the bathroom, washed up, and changed his clothes.

Before he settled into bed, he knelt, put his head in his hands, and gave thanks to his father for the blessings and the challenges that lay before him. That night Josh, slept peacefully with the cool smell of snow wafting into his bedroom from the small crack he left open at his window.

Chapter 5

Tommy and Boarders

The next morning, Josh woke up to a bright blue sky and a light twinkling blanket of snow. He opened his window wide, smiled, took in a big breath of fresh cold air, and looked up to his father, wished him a good morning, and asked for his blessing to bless those he will meet throughout his day.

After he showered and dressed, Josh headed down the stairs stopping briefly at the small landing to look out the window and see the beautiful Lake Superior just beyond the yard and past the train tracks. *What a glorious site.* This was something he missed last night, and he was glad he remembered that Flynn had mentioned something about a view from this widow, so he took a moment to stop and soak it all in.

Downstairs, he found breakfast was served in the dining room. Everyone had a seat, and at each place, there was a different place setting, coffee mug, silverware, juice glass, and a menu standing in a card holder shaped like an autumn leaf. Josh felt a little uncomfortable when he first walked into the dining room.

Everyone at the table looked up in surprise; a fiery red headed woman asked.

"Well where did you come from?" This said the other three boarders looked up from their breakfasts with bewildered faces. Josh took a quick look around the room. He noted that next to the redheaded woman was an elderly gentleman, a middle aged woman, who shyly lowered her head, sat next to him at the head of one end of the table and a young man sat next to an empty seat across from the red headed woman speaking to him as he continued to eat he took in the scene before him.

He smiled a genuine hello and introduced himself.

"My name is Josh Davidson. I arrived later last evening and with Flynn's permission will finish moving in today."

"How long do you plan on staying, Mr. Davidson?" Ginger asked boldly.

"Ginger, George scolded, take it easy on the lad." He smiled at Josh while pointing to the seat across from him. He then reached across the table in a gesture of friendship to shake hands and Josh reciprocated.

"Wow, George said as suddenly pulled his hand away and looked at Josh.

What was that?"

I'm sorry it didn't hurt right?"

"No it was incredible. What exactly was that?" As everyone looked on Josh explained.

"My father told me it was a gift. It's actually different for each person."

"It sure is a gift, Sean you should try this." Josh extended his hand, Sean glimpsed up shrugging his shoulders refused politely.

"Uhm, no, no thank you, it's really nice to meet you though.

"You don't know what you're missing." George mumbled as Ginger playfully swatted his arm. During this encounter Josh

As he did this, he couldn't help but notice the smells of fresh coffee and bacon wafting from the kitchen.

When he sat down at the open spot he realized he was hungrier than he thought. As he reached for the menu, a young man about sixteen years old asked if he would like some coffee.

He smiled warmly at the young man and said, "Yes please, that would be wonderful, regular, thank you."

<hr>

The young man left and returned shortly with a small carafe of coffee, poured his first cup, and said, "Let me know when this is empty, and I'll get you some more."

Josh looked up. "Well, thank you again, and what is your name?"

"Oh, sorry about that. I always forget to tell people my name. My name is Tom."

"Do you live here?" Josh asked inquisitively.

"No, I live next door. Mr. McNamee lets me work for him before and after school. I serve breakfast, and then I come and help with cleaning after school. I started when Mrs. McNamee got sick, and then of course after she died, he needed a lot of help running the place. He pays pretty well too, and I have all of my evenings off. That way, I can do all my homework and still do stuff with my friends."

"Tom," Flynn's voice could be heard from the kitchen.

"Shoot, there I go again talking too much. I gotta go. We can talk later if you'd like."

"I'd like that very much," Josh said. "Maybe after your work and after school?"

"Okay, see ya." Tom disappeared into the kitchen and came back carrying several of the borders' breakfasts, then took Josh's order and disappeared again.

Josh introduced himself and started talking to the other boarders and found out that the couple living across the hall from him was an older couple, George and Ginger Brownstone. They were in their middle sixties. George had a full head of white hair, and Ginger had the larger-than-life personality and fiery red hair; both have been living in Flynn's house for the last two years. They thought about looking for an apartment but decided that this was just perfect for them, and they worked out a special lease with Flynn that helped out both parties.

Sean Roberts, the young gentleman across the table and to his right, was a high school teacher in town. He taught history at the local high school. He was relatively new in town and was also fresh out of college. He seemed very excited about his work and the kids he worked with.

The woman on his left, Florence Beam, was very quiet and forty something. She didn't really have much to interject to the conversation and ate her breakfast mostly in silence. Every so often, she would look up from the newspaper she was reading and smile, then quickly look back down as if afraid someone might ask her to join in the conversation.

After about ten minutes, Josh's breakfast arrived along with a newspaper. He bowed his head to give thanks and marveled at the bounty set before him. He remarked that if he ate like this every morning, running better become one of his rituals each day.

Everyone at the table laughed and continued eating and enjoying their conversation with their newfound friend.

Soon everyone was finished, and Tom came out and asked if anyone needed a travel mug for their coffee or tea to take with them on their way. There was a thunderous yes, and he handed each one a mug with Flynn's Place written on the front. Tom poured them whatever they desired, coffee or tea, and each boarder gave a smile thanked him and headed out the door to start their day.

Chapter 6

Alice

Josh went into the living room and first noticed the fireplace warmly lit with several pictures placed on its mantle. All the pictures were of people smiling, and several had Flynn in them. Josh tried to imagine the stories that went with each picture.

"Those are pictures of my family Flynn said coming up behind Josh. These are pictures of my children and my grandkids. This one here, the black and white one with the young man smiling with that silly grin and that beautiful young girl laughing like there's no tomorrow? That's my favorite one. That's my wife and I on our wedding day. We were so happy that day. Looking back always makes me smile. I miss her a great deal you know."

Josh pointed to the overstuffed sofa facing the fireplace indicating that he'd love to hear more. The two men sat down, and Flynn continued, "Alice and I were so in love we hated being separated. This whole boarding house was her idea you know. After I retired from the insurance company, we decided this is what we would like to do.

She was only able to really work it with me for about five years. Then she started to feel sick. At first, she just started feeling tired and then had difficulty doing even the simplest of things, she lost weight for no reason, and then she found the lump under her arm. We decided to take her to the doctor, and he ran some tests. He said we should take the results and go over to Mayo Clinic in Rochester Minnesota. Have you ever heard of the place?" Josh looking intently at Flynn shook his head no. "No? Well, they're the best. Anyway, we went there to make sure, but it didn't look good." At Mayo, they concluded after several tests that Alice had lymphatic cancer. It was in its advanced stages. They told us that we could start treatments there or go back home and have them here but that the chemotherapy would only make her more comfortable if she was in pain. If she wasn't experiencing pain, then she wouldn't need anything. Her life with all of us was just a matter of time. Luckily for Alice, pain wasn't the problem.

"She really suffered from fatigue and weight loss. This caused a weakness that was nerve-racking for her. She was always such a go-getter. She was miserable to have so many people do for her. But she had to realize that sooner than later, this was the way her life was going to be, and it was best to accept it than to fight it. After one and a half years, the good Lord came and took my beautiful Alice.

"Since then, I've been keeping the boarding house going partly because it was her dream and partly because it gives my life meaning and purpose, something to do I guess. Oh, gosh! I got carried away. I must have bored you to tears. You are very nice to sit here and listen to an old man prattle on when I'm sure you have better things to do with your time."

Josh looked at Flynn squarely in the face, smiled slowly, and took his hand into both of his own. The warmth that flowed from Josh's hands to Flynn's was unexplainable. Then with the same warmth, Josh spoke, "Flynn, I can't think of a better way to spend my morning than to listen to your story and the love you shared with your lovely wife. Thank you."

Flynn, with tears still in his gray, blue eyes, smiled back and said, "Well, you're welcome. Tomorrow maybe we can talk about *you*. I'm sure your life is just as or more interesting as mine."

"Sounds fair. Now can you point me to Harry's Hardware Store. The ad in the paper says that he's looking for a carpenter. I thought after I picked up my few things that I left at the hotel, I'd check it out."

"Oh, are you a carpenter?" asked Flynn.

"Well, really a jack of all trades, but my father taught me carpentry, and I do tend to love that the best of all the trades I do know."

"Okay then, do you remember Jenny's?" Flynn questioned.

"That diner I ate dinner at last night?"

"Yes. Good, go past the diner. Cross the street. You'll see the Opera House, then a little coffee house, next to a Starbucks and a bookstore Kate's Novel-Tea-Nook. Across that street, you'll see Harry's Hardware Store. When you get there tell him Flynn sent you and that you're staying at my place."

"Hey, thanks, Flynn, that means a lot to me."

"It'll mean a lot to Harry too. Also, don't worry about your things at the motel. I'll send Tommy over after school."

"He won't mind?"

"Nope, not at all. He's a good boy, loves to do for others. I don't know what I'd do without him, a real blessing that boy is." Flynn smiled back. "Now go on. Get going before someone else gets that job before you."

Josh finished his coffee, looked for a place to set his cup down, and settled on handing it to Flynn. He smiled, threw his coat on, said thanks again, and ran out the door. Flynn just shook his head and walked back to the kitchen with both his and Josh's coffee mugs. *That Josh sure is electrifying,* thought Flynn. *That smile, those eyes, and his touch, you just can't describe the feeling. Well, it sure is different,* he said to himself.

Chapter 7

Harry

The brisk wind hit Josh in the face like a burst of cold air from a freezer on a one-hundred-degree day. *Boy it's chilly out here*, he thought. *I have to remember to get a scarf, hat, and gloves today.*

Everything looked beautiful. There was a dusting of snow all over, and as if on cue, a light snow began to fall softly all around him. Soon he was at Harry's Hardware. Josh looked up and noticed that it was an old brick building with a nice front window decorated with the all things autumn. There were colored leaves, a basket filled with plastic red and green apples, a rake in the corner, and a few bright orange pumpkins leaning up against a hay bale. As he walked in, a little bell rang over the door, and he asked the gentleman behind the paint counter wearing a plaid flannel shirt and denim coveralls, "Are you Harry?"

"Me? No. No, sir," the man said. "My name is Billy."

"Oh. I'm sorry may I speak with Harry?"

"Sure fella just a minute. Are you here to ask for the job in the paper?"

Josh smiled and said, "Yes, I am, if it's still available." Billy looked Josh over. Josh was wearing his leather jacket with a blue oxford shirt, tan khaki pants, and brown loafers.

"Sure is, but if ya ask me, you don't look much like a carpenter."

"Well, my father taught me everything I know, and I've been doing carpentry on my own for the last ten years or so online. Is Harry here? I would really like to speak with him if I could."

"Sure, sure, just a minute." Billy nodded. "I'll be right back with him. He's in the back working on some bills."

"Okay, thanks. I'll wait right here," Josh said. After a few minutes, Josh looked up as he heard someone walking toward him.

"Bill here tells me you're interested in the carpentry job," Harry said as he came from the back of the store reaching out to shake Josh's hand. "I'm Harry, and you are?"

"I'm Josh, Josh Davidson," he replied as he grabbed Harry's hand firmly. Harry stepped back as the electrifying feeling he shared with Josh warmed his hand and filled his head with wonderful memories as their hands connected. Josh smiled at him, and Harry let go, and the feeling ended just as quickly as it began. Harry looked up at Josh, smiled, looked at his hand, and started to say something, but Josh grinned openly and said, "Weird, right? It's a gift, at least my father tells me it is."

"I can't ever remember a feeling like that, ever," Harry said scratching his head. He stumbled over his words as he tried to regain his composure. Looking at his hand, he just stared at it in surprise, then looked at Billy, then back at Josh and tried to smile.

"Uh, Bi-Billy here also tells me that you're experienced as well." Josh looked at Harry and Billy thoughtfully while nodding yes.

"Yes, sir, I am. I saw your ad in this morning's paper and thought I'd check it out. My father was a carpenter, and he trained me from the time I was a little boy. Are you still hiring, or am I too late?"

Well, we had one young fellow come in earlier, but I haven't had the opportunity to look up any of his credentials yet. Have you any credentials I can call or look at?"

"Um, I don't really like to be a namedropper, but I could really use this job."

"Go on," Harry said. "Who should I contact?"

"Okay, well, my landlord Flynn McNamee did tell me to mention his name and said that if you wanted to call him you could."

The two older men exchanged glances, and Harry shook his head and said, "Good old Flynn." Then Harry absently rubbed his neck.

"Flynn sent you?"

"Yes, he did," Josh said giving a winning smile.

"You see, Flynn and me, we go back a long way," Harry explained.

"If he sent you and you have some experience."

"Yes. If you'd like, I can bring my album of work that I have, or if you have a computer, I can give you the disk I brought to pop in for you to see my work."

"You know how to work computers too?" Bill interjected.

"Yes, I guess a little. Do you need help with something?"

"Well, you see Bill here and I don't know too much about these darn here computers. So maybe if I hire you, maybe you can help us learn that, as well as do the specialty carpentry items I'll need help with."

"Sure, no problem," Josh offered. "Here let me get you started with the disk I brought and give you some time to look at it while I go to Jenny's for a quick lunch. Then I'll come back, and you can let me know about the job. How does that sound?"

Harry and Bill looked at each other, and Harry agreed, "That sounded like a good idea." Josh showed the two men how to work the computer after he placed his disk into it. As he was walking out the door, he could hear the two men praising his work.

Chapter 8

Maggie Stone

The wind had picked up; the snow was falling a bit heavier and was starting to accumulate. Josh felt a sudden urgency to at least get a hat and gloves. So instead of the diner, he made a beeline to the corner Ben Franklin apparel store. Once inside, there was the excitement that the first a heavy snowfall of the season brings with it in everyone's behavior. People were rushing to buy coats, gloves, hats, scarves, and boots. Some were even buying crafts to work on while they would be snow-bound.

Josh looked out the window and across the street; the Super Mart's parking lot was filling up. People were rushing to get provisions in case they got stuck inside for a few days. Josh got pensive at the thought. The thought of families staying home together as the first winter storm covered their homes and property with a blanket of snow warmed his heart. He just couldn't help it.

Let's see, he thought, *I came here for a hat and gloves*. He picked up a brown knit cap and a pair of leather and knit gloves. He also thought with this being the first snow, maybe he should get some snow pants, a parka, mittens, a scarf, and boots. *This way, I can help with snow removal when necessary.*

After gathering all of his new apparel, he went up to the register and got in line behind a young woman who was buying just a few things.

Her son and little girl were with her, and he overheard the boy say, "Mom, I *need* the snow pants *and* boots. Mine don't fit any more."

"*Sh*, Jimmy, you know we can't afford those now. You'll just have to wear what we have."

"But, Mom, the boots hurt my feet, and they have a hole. Please, Mom."

"No, Jimmy, you heard me."

"Yes, Mom, I guess so, sorry."

"Excuse me, I couldn't help but overhear," Josh interjected.

"Oh I'm sorry if we bothered you." The woman glared at her son.

"No, not at all," Josh insisted. "My name is Josh. Would you mind if we stepped out of the line for just a second?"

"Uh, well, I don't know," the woman said as she lowered her eyes to the floor. "I really need to get going, and I really don't know you."

"Of course, let me explain. As I said I did overhear your dilemma, and I was wondering if you would mind terribly if I helped you out."

"Help me out? How? Why?"

"I just thought you seem to be a little short on cash right now. If you aren't, then I apologize for being a busybody, but if you need help, I'm in the position to do that."

"At what cost?" Maggie looked up at him warily. Then frustratingly, she asked, "I mean what do you want for the money?"

"Nothing, just knowing that your children are well protected against the cold and snow is payment enough."

"*Really?*" She looked at him again quizzically.

"Really, please I would consider it an honor to help you out."

At the same time, Jimmy started pulling on his mom's coat and pleading, "*Please, Mom, please* let this man help us just this once, *please.*"

Josh looked at the boy, then looked at the woman and smiled and begged, "Yeah, *please, Mom, please.*" His hands were clasped in front of him.

She couldn't help but start laughing and said, "Oh, all right, but just this once, and I plan to pay you back as soon as I can. I promise. Where do you live?" Maggie asked.

Josh tried to wave the agreement away but realized she was not joking and suddenly becoming serious and said, "Absolutely, I'm living at Flynn's. How about we figure out a payment plan starting as soon as the spring's thaw."

"All right, but first, let's start over again." She put her hand out to shake Josh's. "My name's Maggie, Maggie Stone. It's nice to meet you."

Josh extended his hand and smiled and said, "Nice to meet you, Maggie, my name's Josh Davidson." At the touch of Josh's hand, Maggie's breath was taken away. She looked at her hand; then she looked at Josh. She quickly released his hand and tried to hide her embarrassment, asking, "What *was* that?"

Josh continued smiling and playfully asked back, "What was what?"

"You know what. What was that, that feeling?"

"Oh that, well, that happens a lot. I don't really have a good explanation for it. It's just something that happens when I make a connection with someone."

"Well, just so you know, I'm married to a marine, and he's in Afghanistan right now, and I have no desire to do anything to hurt him or my marriage."

"And just so that you know, I would never even attempt to come between you and your husband. That is the last thing on my mind. We're just friends, okay?"

"Okay."

"Good, then let's go look at those boots and snow pants." By the time they got through the register line, the little boy, little girl, and mother all had new winter jackets, hats, gloves, scarves, snow pants, and boots. Josh had his hat, gloves, parka, snow pants, mittens, boots, and a ski vest to wear to boot. Josh gave Maggie his phone number. Once Maggie finagled the receipt from Josh, she pledged to pay back every red cent he'd spent on them excluding the jackets and things for her and the daughter. They were gifts from him and his idea. The deal was struck, and everyone was happy.

Josh told Maggie that if she ever needed anything, she could get in touch with him by using that phone number. She agreed and extended the same courtesy. She already knew Flynn and felt better knowing that at least someone she knew also knew this kind and generous man. God had truly blessed her today. She would surely remember this in her prayers tonight. Jimmy couldn't believe what had happened today. Maybe what he had heard about guardian angels and miracles in his religion classes was really true. If he didn't believe in miracles before, today would be the beginning of his belief in them.

Josh had spent a great deal of time in the Ben Franklin more than he had planned, so instead of grabbing lunch, he went straight back to Harry's Hardware. There he found Harry behind the register counting out the drawer.

Harry looked up and smiled. "Going to be a big one today. We're going to close up shop early. Looks like you got yourself an armful of winter wear."

"I sure did, figured I'd need a few things if I'm sticking around. *Am* I sticking around, Harry?"

"How would I, oh you mean the job, right?"

"Yep, I was wondering if you had the time to look at my work and call Flynn. I know with the snow and all you've probably been pretty busy."

Harry rubbed the back of his neck and looked at Josh and said, "You know, boy, Billy and I were mighty impressed. You're awfully talented. Are you sure you want to work here? I mean we may not have enough work for you, and I'm not sure we can pay you enough either."

"You don't have to worry about that," Josh exclaimed. "I can do your orders and if you don't mind I can set up a website and do special orders off that in the back work room. You won't even have to pay me for those orders. How does that sound?"

"Well, it sounds like a match made in heaven if you ask me." Josh stuck out his hand, and Harry reluctantly reached out across the counter, and the two shook hands in agreement, and there it was again, that feeling. *Wow!* It just made him feel so wonderful. Still how could he explain it? He just didn't know. As he looked at their hands, he noticed Josh staring at them and became a little self-conscious and sheepishly loosened his grip. Realizing Harry's discomfort, Josh pointed outside and suggested that he head back to Flynn's before it gets too deep. Josh thanked Harry and asked when he should report to work.

"We're pretty relaxed around here especially around this time of year. Can I give you a call when this snow lets up? I know Flynn's number. I'll call then. Does that sound okay to you?"

"That sounds better than okay. Thanks again, Harry, take care, and be safe out there."

"You too, Josh," Harry said getting back to his closing tasks.

<hr>

Josh couldn't even see across the square to the movie house. The snow was so thick, and the flakes were as big as silver dollars. He had never seen snow before. Come to think of it, he had never really seen snow before period. *Amazing.* Josh stopped where he was and closed his eyes and took a moment to thank his Heavenly Father for this spectacular *change* of events with employment and for the miracle that happened when cold air and water mix with each other. Our God is certainly clever to have created something so beautiful.

Chapter 9

Kate Ryan

Before he went any further, Josh noticed that a small store still had its lights on. With the open sign still turned, maybe he could put some of his newly bought treasures on to protect him from the elements outside. He quickly ran down a few stores and jumped inside. He shook himself and saw that he was in a quant, little bookstore. The young woman behind the counter was counting down her drawer and held one finger up to him so that he didn't disturb her counting. Josh complied and continued to look around and brush the remainder of snow off his jacket.

The woman slowly looked up, smiled, and said thank you.

"You have no idea how many times I've had to count that. My name is Kate, Kate Ryan," she said as she walked around the counter to greet him.

Kate is twenty-eight years old and just recently acquired the Novel-Tea-Nook Bookstore. She stands about five feet, three inches and has beautiful auburn hair and piercing blue eyes.

"Now what can I do for you?"

"My name is Josh. Nice to meet you. You have a great place here. It's very homey."

"Thank you." Kate smiled as she looked up to Josh standing over her at just six feet tall. "Can I help you with something? I just closed the drawer. With the storm and all, I'm closing early."

"No, that's okay. I'm a little embarrassed. I noticed your lights on and thought I'd quickly come in and put some of my new outer wear on before I head back to Flynn's."

"Oh well, while you're here, would you like a tour? Like I said I'm a little slow and the place isn't very big, so I can give you the royal tour."

"Great." Josh smiled back. "I'd love that."

"You're new around here, right?" she asked with her bright blue eyes taking in Josh's face and height.

"Yes, I just got a place over at Flynn's last night."

"Really? He's very picky. You must be very special."

"I don't know about that," Josh interjected, "but he sure is a nice guy."

"I just got a job over at Harry's also."

"Harry's Hardware? Well, *you are special*," Kate said as she gave Josh the once over. "Harry is no pushover. Did you know he's the mayor as well?"

Josh looked at Kate shocked. "Uh, no I didn't. He didn't say anything to me about that at all."

Kate smiled sheepishly and said, "No, he doesn't like to reveal his true identity. It's a small town. He probably figured that Flynn would eventually tell you."

"It's a small bookstore," Kate continued. "We have a section here of all new books. And this section here by the fireplace is where we have the some of the classics. The knitting group meets every Friday afternoon, and the Wednesday morning book club meets here too.

"We have professors that meet here on Thursday nights to have their book discussions. They come from the surrounding junior college and two universities. That night is always interesting with very lengthy discussions.

"On the third Friday of the month, we have a 'Meet the Author' afternoon tea and evening book signing. Every other Friday night is open mic nights."

"Sometimes we have local authors or new authors come in and talk about their books. They answer questions and do book signings. The open mic nights are for local talent. The kids from the colleges and the local high school really get involved.

"Saturday evenings are pajama night for the kids. Here's a sheet that gives all the listings for the month there's a new one every month."

"This is very nice," Josh exclaimed as he gratefully took the sheet from Kate and put it in his jacket pocket.

• ━━━━━━━━━⌒━━━━━ •

While surveying the store further, Josh also noticed that Kate used all kinds of things to shelve her books. Some were on old step ladders.

Some books were stacked neatly on top of each other on the floor. Other books were on tables and in baskets. It really was a unique kind of store.

At the front of the store she showed him an area that was for used books.

"How do you get the used books?" Josh asked.

"I get a lot donated from people in town, and the money from those goes to different charities each month. Then the ones that are marked with red stickers are on consignment. I sell all of the hardbacks for five dollars and all the paperbacks for one dollar. I have to add tax of course but after that I split the earnings with the person who brought the book in. Sometimes it's a win-win situation sometimes they end up just donating. Even then, I think it works out all right," Kate said thoughtfully.

"So what's your story? Just trying to get in from the storm or looking for a book?" Josh was surprised at her bluntness but also found it uniquely interesting.

Standing there a little embarrassed, he knew he had to be honest.

"As I said I was just coming in actually to change from my shoes to my boots and my leather jacket to my down jacket. I'm afraid I don't have an interesting reason, actually it's a little lame really."

"Not really, I think it was a good idea since most of the stores are closed. Can I ask why you didn't do this at home before you left? Wouldn't it have been easier?" she queried.

"Yes, except that I just bought all these things at the Ben Franklin. I'm afraid the storm caught me a bit off guard," Josh explained.

Kate shook her head and said, "Just to let you know here in Munising, as close as we are to Thanksgiving, these little storms pop up out of nowhere all the time, so you always need to be prepared."

"Thanks for the advice." Josh gave a little wink. "I'll try to remember it. For now though, I think I should get going while I can still get across town without a snowmobile. How about you? How are you getting home?" Josh was just curious. "You're not driving, are you?"

"No. I just live up the stairs. It's great for days like this, not, however, for days when people are doing research in the middle of the night." They shared a laugh and shook hands. Kate froze and quickly took her hand away. She looked up at Josh and said, "That was quite a shock. What do you call that trick?" Josh was surprised he didn't really understand what she meant.

"Excuse me? What do you mean?"

"I mean I've never experienced anything like that when shaking someone's hand. How did you do that?"

"Oh, that shock or feeling you had?"

"Yes, was that some kind of trick?" Josh lowered his eyes and shook his head

"No, no trick. It's just the way my inner self connects with others."

Kate looked at him intently and said, "Well, maybe when you have time, we can discuss it over tea."

"That would be great," Josh said relieved not to have to further explain himself. It was nice meeting you Kate. I'm sure I'll be back soon. I love reading, and I love your store."

"Great, it was nice meeting you too, Josh. I look forward to seeing you again."

"That sounds great, for now, I better go brave the whipping winds of the North." As Josh walked out the door, Kate peeked past the curtains as she turned her Open sign to shut. She couldn't stop thinking about that weird feeling she got when she shook his hand. She looked out the window again, but now all she saw was snow and more snow. *This blizzard was going to be a big one. I hope he knows his way back home*, Kate thought as she started turning lights off and heading upstairs to her cozy little apartment with Gabby, her Calico cat, following close behind, hoping her husband Mac wouldn't have trouble getting back from the university.

Chapter 10

The Snow

Once again, Josh headed out the door to a very strong north wind. It was very quiet as no cars were on the roads. Josh passed a few kids playing in the snow on his right, and just as he thought, he made a wrong turn somewhere. He looked across the street. Through the all the white in front of him, he could barely make out the lights on the brick porch and the light on in the little telephone room of Flynn's. He was very happy because he was just beginning to feel the cold stinging his face as the wind continued to whip all around him.

———◦———

Flynn, watching Josh carefully crossing the highway, opened the door for him as he stepped up on the porch and helped him in. He helped him out of his coat and, ushering him into the foyer, noticed his bag and gave him a questioning look. Josh, shrugging out of his parka, explained that he had stopped in to the Novel-Tea-Nook to change his outer gear and met Kate. She gave him a bag to help carry some of his belongings.

He explained that he had received the grand tour before heading out into the storm.

Flynn smiled and said, "Ah yes."

"Kate is very proud of her place. She and her husband had just acquired it and put a great deal of work into it."

"You can tell. It looks very different than other bookstores, very eclectic and homey at the same time," Josh mentioned.

"How did the job inquiry go at Harry's?"

"Great!" Josh exclaimed excitedly. "He was a little worried at first with my experience and amount of work to do. But I assured him that I was more than happy to work with him on a salary if I could use the workroom in back to handle my web accounts as well. We agreed and he said we could work out the details sometime after the storm. He was closing early and said he'd give me a call later.

"By the way, I assume he called for a reference so thank you for that. I know that we don't know each other well, actually at all..."

"Don't mention it, Josh, I know what it's like just starting out in a new town not knowing anybody. I'm just glad I could be of help. Don't let me live to regret it," he said looking at Josh with a sideways glance.

"Oh, I won't. I just hope I can live up to Harry's expectations."

"I'm sure you won't have trouble with that. Harry's a good guy and very easy going," Flynn said, slapping Josh on the back, leading him toward the living room.

In the living room, Josh noticed that the elderly couple and the teacher he had met earlier were already in there.

They each had a cup of cocoa and were playing a game of scrabble in front of the roaring fire in the fireplace. On the sidecar table were thermoses of hot coffee, hot cocoa, and hot water for tea, along with some cookies and crackers for everyone. As he walked in, he grabbed a mug of cocoa and a handful of cookies before joining the group by the fireplace. Standing there, the storm going on out the window caught his eye. He couldn't help but stare in wonder and amazement at how the power of the wind and the gentleness of the snow could so easily wreak havoc on such a community. In awe of what was before him Josh silently prayed.

> *"Dear Father please give safe passage to those struggling to get home to their loved ones. Thank you so much for the protection you have provided me with. Lastly thank you for the warm friendships I am developing and sharing.*
>
> *Amen*

Soon he was being taken in by the laughter and conversation of the couple playing a board game.

"Josh, George asked, do you know how to spell glorious? Do I need another "o" after the "u" and before the "s"?"

"What are you playing?"

We're playing a word game called Scrabble." Ginger explained

"No George you do not need another "o" it's spelled glorious." Josh spelled.

"Yeah hey! Got you Red," George said playfully.

"I won."

"You sure did good looking, would you like to play again? Ginger questioned teasingly.

"Josh would you like to join us and cozy up to the fireplace for a while?" Ginger suggested.

"Warming up to the fire sounds wonderful but instead of playing I'd rather watch first if you don't mind."

"It's fine by us, right sweetie." Ginger smiled lovingly at her husband as he nodded approvingly.

After a while Flynn came in wearing his bright orange vest.

"Hey everybody, I'm going to walk over to the Grocer's across the way to pick up a few provisions. You never know, this early snowstorm could get worse before it gets better. One thing we don't want is to be caught without the necessities of life." Josh and Sean looked at each other as if they were one person. In unison they said.

"We'll go for you." Josh stated.

"That's right; Josh and I can take your list and run there and back in no time. Why don't you stay here with George and Ginger?"

"That's a great idea Flynn. Let the young ones go out there." Ginger agreed. Flynn protested.

"I love this kind of weather. What's wrong with everybody? Do you think I'm too old or something?

"No." everyone chimed in.

"It's just a little snow after all" Flynn said defiantly.

"We just wanted to help." Josh retorted.

"O.k.," Flynn gave in.

If you boys want to keep me company while carrying the groceries home that would be great."

The three donned their winter clothes and boots. Next, they made sure all of them had working cell phones.

Ginger walked to the door with them and told them to be careful and to call when they got to the store. "I worry you know. It's not safe out there. Why don't you wait until it lets up a bit then go," Ginger said exasperated.

"If we wait too long, we won't have any provisions *to get*. They'll be gone, and it could be days before they can get a truck in here for the grocery stores," Flynn replied

"Oh all right, just promise me that you'll call when you get there."

George came up behind Ginger and wrapped her in his arms and grinned. "She sure is a keeper, isn't she? She's the biggest worrier in the North."

"George!" Ginger snapped as she swiped playfully at his shoulder and wrapped her arms around his swaying in his gentleness. Quickly, the men scurried out the door so as not to let the snow and wind blow in behind them.

As the three men were walking, they all realized that Ginger had reason to worry. Flynn hadn't seen a storm like this in years. Even though Sean was from the Chicago land area, he thought this was by far more snow than he'd ever seen, and Josh, well, being from a warmer climate, had never seen this kind of weather before. They finally made it to the grocer's, and Flynn thought, by the looks of it, it was just in the nick of time.

So much of the food was gone that the store looked like it was going out of business. More shelves than not were empty, and the lines at the registers' were five and six people deep. They called Ginger as soon as they remembered and then set out to gather what they could to make sure there was enough food for everyone for the next day or two if necessary. Although in two days, it would be Thanksgiving, and Flynn was already prepared for that day. He had shopped for the holiday well in advance as well as most people in the town of Munising. Their shopping for that day had been at least a week in the past by now. So having food for that day is not the worry. It's in having the basics that's concerning these people—the basics meaning, milk, eggs, toilet paper, and bread; anything else would be supplies in case of electrical outages or gas outages.

Josh, Sean, and Flynn quickly got to work and used the divide and conquer method and promised to meet at the checkout counters in approximately fifteen minutes. With that decided, Josh went off to get flashlights, batteries, candles, and quick-lite lighters for the candles. Sean headed toward the toilet paper and bread aisles. Flynn decided to get the eggs, milk, and butter. When they each finished their task, they met at the checkout lanes and shortly found themselves outside in the elements again.

On their way home, the men didn't even try to have a conversation. The wind was so strong and cold it took their breath away. All three put their shoulders into the wind and forged ahead as though they were defensive linebackers holding the offensive team back from scoring the winning touchdown. The visibility was only about six inches in front of them.

Flynn thought to himself, *This is going to break all kinds of records here in Munising and in the state of Michigan as well.* The snow had accumulated to approximately two feet in the last two and a half hours, and it didn't look as though there was any sign of it letting up any time soon.

———

Ginger was standing in the telephone room watching for the three of them and worrying the whole while. George came in carrying a fresh cup of cocoa and words of encouragement to share. Then he left her to check on the weather. She still continued to keep her vigil until she could see the bright-orange vest that Flynn insists on wearing in weather like this.

"You never know this old vest just might save my life sometime. The snow gets pretty thick. I want to make sure that I'm seen from all angles." Ginger could here Flynn commenting on that old vest as if he were standing right there in the room with her. It made her smile when she thought about it.

Even though Ginger had difficulty seeing through the storm, she never once took her eyes off the highway that runs directly in front of Flynn's Boarding House.

She had just looked at her watch and yelled to George, "Is it really 5:45? I'm really starting to worry. Oh, wait is that them? Come here. See if that's them. You know how my eyes are."

"Hurry up, *George,* for goodness' sake. What's taking you so long?"

"I was just grabbing a few crackers. I'm right here. Yep, yep that's them all right.

I can see that old bright vest of Flynn's. Boy, that thing sure isn't hard to miss."

"Stop it!" Ginger admonished. "Thank God he's got that crazy thing."

"Let's get some blankets ready and check the cocoa thermos, make sure there is enough in there for the three of them. The blankets are in that bench right there on the porch." George went to the porch and pulled out three heavy quilts and brought them to the living room and set them in front of the fireplace on the couch to warm up. Ginger checked the thermos and found that there was plenty there for at least three cups of cocoa.

Just as they were meeting in the phone room, Flynn, Josh, and Sean burst through the door. Ginger and George quickly ushered them inside and took the groceries while the three men brushed the heavy snow off their coats and shook it from their heads. Next, they took all their wet clothing off and hung them on a tree stand. George and Ginger took the groceries and put them into the kitchen on the kitchen table. Ginger put the eggs and bread away in the refrigerator.

Once all there outer clothing was off and drying, Flynn, Josh, and Sean grabbed mugs of cocoa, wrapped themselves in blankets, and sat down in front of the fireplace to warm up. Ginger and George joined them in the living room pulling up and sitting in the two overstuffed leather chairs that usually frame the picture window. The five of them sat and talked until 7:00.

Josh was warming up when he realized that someone was missing.

"Has anyone seen or heard from Ms.Beam today?" Asked Josh.

"Yes," Ginger sat up straighter.

"She called earlier as the storm was just starting. She told me she was with friends and would stay with them until the storm ended or overnight if need be. She said to lock up that she has her key." Suddenly Flynn slapped his legs asking is anyone hungry? All four boarders turned in his direction and exclaimed a rousing yes! With that He stood up and started heading toward the kitchen. Josh following close behind asked.

"May I help you?" Flynn turned to see Josh standing there grinning said,

"Of course you can, the more the merrier." Walking together Josh inquired,

"What do you think you're going to make?"

"A little dish we call Chili. "

"How do you make that? What ingredients do you use?"

"I use an old family recipe. I use hamburger, kidney beans, stewed tomatoes, onions. tomato sauce, and tomato soup. I brown the hamburger and the onions. Then mix it with the rest of the ingredients and let it simmer on the stove until we're ready to eat."

"That sounds delicious." Josh thought out loud."

"Well let's start cooking!" Flynn said with a flourish.

"This is just the ticket for a night like this," Flynn said as he started chopping the onions and as Josh threw the kidney beans in.

Once all the ingredients were in the pot, simmering on the stove and the corn bread was slid into the oven Josh excused himself and headed upstairs to change into more comfortable clothing to settle in for the night

At the same time Sean stood and watched out the picture window as the snow continued to fall. Ginger now content knowing the three had made it home safely was chatting animatedly with George while sitting in front of the fireplace. The boardinghouse and its boarders were content and warm for the snowy evening ahead of them.

Chapter 11

Flynn Remembers

Flynn went through the mudroom, grabbed a jacket, and headed out the back door to his little house just behind the boarding house. Flynn loved this little house that sat behind the bigger house with its kitchen, 2 bedrooms, and living room. It was perfect for him, just the right size. It used to be a guestroom for people who were looking for an overnight place. He and his wife would rent it out like a bed-and-breakfast. However, when Flynn's wife died, he decided that he would just move into the little house and scoot between both during the day. In the evening, he would then have his privacy, time to himself, and a place to work on his bills and menus for the boarders.

As he walked inside, he smiled to himself, took off his jacket, turned on the fire, grateful that he had converted it into a gas fireplace, sat down in his favorite chair, turned, and took a look out the small front window. He saw that

Tommy was revving up the snow blower getting ready to start clearing the driveway and walkway from his house to Tommy's. He had already cleared a path between the big house and his little house.

He smiled to himself remembering his conversation with his Alice about hiring this nice, *young boy* as she often called him, just to help out. At that time, Tommy was just thirteen years old. He was all bright eyes and so eager to help. He started just after school; then as Alice began to get sicker, he came more and more often. He'd run an errand or two; then, he'd help her on and off the sofa, then well to what he is now, three years later. A *young man* helping in the morning with breakfast, snow shoveling, mowing, errand-running, and anything else he asked.

What a kid, don't know what I'd do without him, Flynn thought as he shook his head. Flynn went into the kitchen and grabbed the cookbook with the best recipes for Thanksgiving side dishes since it was only days away, put his jacket back on, and headed back to the big house. As he walked, he waved at Tommy, and Tommy smiled and waved back as he continued to blow the snow into mounds along the sides of the driveway.

Chapter 12

The Search

Waiting in the kitchen for Flynn were four anxious adults talking amongst themselves. They all looked up when he walked in.

"What's up? Flynn asked as he hung his jacket in the mudroom. You all look as though someone just died. No, did I just put my foot in my mouth? Did someone die?"

"No, but we do have a problem," Josh spoke up solemnly. "Do you remember the little boy named Jimmy Stone?"

"Jimmy Stone, Maggie's little boy. Yeah, of course, I know Jimmy. Why?"

"Well," they all said together.

"Well, what's the problem?"

"It appears that little Jimmy went out to play in some new winter clothes he got today and hasn't been seen since," Ginger interjected. Josh looked at Ginger, and a feeling of despair and guilt washed over him, knowing it was he that bought Jimmy those new clothes.

"What do ya mean hasn't been seen since? He didn't just disappear," Flynn said as he looked at each face incredulously.

"Well," Josh continued, "apparently, Maggie was watching him from her kitchen window as he was building a snowman. Then she went to get his sister from her crib. When she went back to the window, he was gone. She went out and started yelling for him, but the snow was too thick and heavy.

"They've started a search party."

"They called in the surrounding towns, but they can't get through. So anyone that's available is supposed to meet over at the diner," Ginger continued.

"They've set up a command center there. We're also asked to bring blankets and flashlights," George finished.

Just as Flynn was about to spring into action, Tommy walked into the back door carrying two blankets, two flashlights, and one lantern. "Did ya hear?" Tommy asked breathlessly. As they all shook their heads, they sprang into action. Ginger ran off to the living room and grabbed the three quilts on the sofa that earlier had warmed Flynn, Josh, and Sean. Flynn and George went downstairs and found a couple of lanterns; Sean went into the garage and found three flashlights. Josh went upstairs and looked in the closet that Flynn directed him to for batteries. He found two packages. He also took this moment to step into his room to say a brief prayer to his father.

Flynn, Ginger, George, Sean, and Tommy had gathered in the foyer and were boxing up the supplies as Josh descended the stairway. Once they all had their winter gear on, they headed out to the van of Tommy's parent. Tommy's father, Andy, helped everyone in.

As they reached Jenny's Diner, no one would never know it was 8:00 in the evening. There were all kinds of commotion going on inside. The snow was slowing down. The wind, however, was picking up, and the temperature was dropping. Finding the boy soon was crucial.

Maggie was over at the counter with Jenny. She was holding a steaming mug of tea and crying. Jenny was consoling her and rubbing her back, helping to keep her calm. Amber was manning the coffee station, making sure there were plenty of hot coffee and hot chocolate as well as cookies available for all the volunteers.

Ginger jumped right in to see where Ally, Maggie's little girl, were at. George, Flynn, Josh, Sean, and Tommy went to the table where several people were standing.

Harry turned around and shook each one's hand and introduced them to Pat Shepherd the sheriff from the county's sheriff department. Pat gave a somber smile and a nod to each.

They then showed the volunteers the map and where they had already sent out search parties. Next, he pointed to an area on the map that wasn't too far from the home but was a little difficult to get around in and was perfect for a group of their size. It's a pretty thick area, lots of trees, both standing and on the ground. "Maggie told us that Jimmy loves to play in there, and maybe he wandered in there and got lost because of the snow."

Sean asked, "Hasn't anyone gone in there yet? Wouldn't that have been the first place someone would have looked?"

"Yes, they did, and yes, it is. However, because of the thickness and quick accumulation of the snow, the group couldn't get very far. But now that the snow is starting to taper off some, we want to reexamine that area again and see if we can get further into that woodsy section," Pat explained.

"Now we hope he didn't wander back there because there's lots of wild life back there too. Remember, people, time is of the essence. It's only getting colder, darker, and more dangerous out there, so let's work sure but fast."

Harry and the sheriff wished them luck. The four of them went over to Maggie to let them know that they would do their very best to bring Jimmy home. With Thanksgiving only two days away, they were anxious to work fast and bring Jimmy to the safety and warmth of his mother and family. Maggie tried to smile but suddenly broke down and started sobbing at the thought of her little boy out there all alone.

Josh asked them for one more thing before they began their search.

"Please can we each take a hand and bow our heads." The group grabbed hands, bowed their heads, and, in a circle, listened as Josh prayed:

> Almighty Father in heaven, we ask that you please protect Jimmy from the elements of the cold and windy weather. We ask that you send an angel to protect him from harm until the searchers are able to find him and return him to his mother, family, and community of friends that are so concerned for his safety. Please, Father, have the Holy Spirit guide us to a swift rescue and reunite Jimmy with all who are praying for his safe return. We ask

that even though we so many times find
your will difficult to understand at first
that through prayer and contemplation
we will come to a greater knowledge of
your almighty plan."

All those in the room responded with a unanimous amen.

Tommy turned to Josh with a questioning look and asked, "What just happened, Josh?"

"What do you mean, Tom? We just said a prayer asking our father to help us on our search for Jimmy."

"No," Tommy said shaking his head. "I mean when I held your hand. That feeling. It like took my breath away. It was the greatest feeling I've ever felt. I can't even describe it. How did you do that?"

"Oh, that." Josh smiled as he looked at Tommy. "It's very difficult to explain. My father says it's a gift."

"It sure is, wow. Does it happen every time someone shakes your hand? Or whenever someone touches you?" Tommy questioned.

"Pretty much every time someone touches me," Josh responded. Now we better hurry. It's not getting any better outside, and there's a little boy waiting for us to find him."

Tommy agreed and, while rubbing his hand, turned with Josh to start the search with the other men.

Harry handed out flashlights and lanterns. Pat Shepherd, the only sheriff police officer that could get through in the county, was at one of the tables handing out maps and making sure that every group had hand held radios for communication. Each group had to have at least have four people, and they were designated a specific area to cover. They were told to give their coordinates every twenty minutes to the command center; they were to be back or at least heading back to the command center within the hour to regroup, warm up, and they were never, ever to separate. These rules were not to be broken under any circumstances.

Soon Josh, Flynn, Tommy, and Sean were on their way. As they left, Kate and Mac walked in and immediately went over to Maggie. Ginger stayed back to help Jenny and Amber replenished the nourishment and warm drinks for the searchers consoling Maggie and helping with Ally. George, Harry, Pat Shepherd, and Tommy's father, Andy, stayed back to listen to radio reports and track the searchers on the map. Josh and his guys were given the area directly behind Maggie's house. These woods are very dense with trees and had a steep incline.

As the men and Tommy climbed, they were grateful that the snow had slowed down. After they had reached the top of the hill, the moon came out of the clouds and brightened up the forest enough so that the men could just slightly see a small clearing off to their right. They decided to head in that direction thinking that maybe Jimmy had a little area over there that he liked to play in. They had been told that this area had been checked once already, but with the snow so thick before and the cloud coverage, something may have been missed. Inside the woods, Tommy thought the silence was eerie.

The rest smiled and Josh said, "Maybe you mean peaceful and calm."

Tommy thought for a moment, laughed, then shook his head. "Nope eerie."

The rest laughed, and they all kept on walking. Every so often, they would hear a tree crack or a scamper of a small animal. These sounds would make them turn their flashlights in different directions and start their hearts beating a little faster. Each time, they would become a little more discouraged when they realized that the sounds were just rabbits or woodsy sounds.

As time went on, they were beginning to feel the cold. Josh was definitely grateful for the warm clothing he had bought earlier. Although it gave him a heavy heart to think that maybe if he hadn't bought the clothes for Jimmy, all of this might not have happened.

Although, he also knew that everything happens for a reason, and maybe the clothes were meant for something good and not so much the reason for the incident.

After twenty minutes, the men radioed in and gave their location. They then explained that they were going to take a short break and have some coffee to warm up and regroup. They said they would radio in when they planned to start searching again.

While Josh and Flynn found some deserted logs to sit on, Sean and Tommy poured the coffee and got some cookies out of their backpacks. While sitting, they discussed their next strategy. They decided to head straight for a few more yards and then turn off to the left where they just happened to see another clearing.

Sean shook his head though and said, "This is already a little too far. After all, he is just a little boy. How far could he have strayed?"

"Well, that's the whole point of this, isn't it?" asked Tommy. "I mean, that's why he's lost. That's why we're looking for him, right?"

"You're right. I know, but it just seems…" Sean's voice trailed off. "Well, I guess I'm just feeling a little discouraged."

"We all are," Flynn chimed in, "but we can't let that get the better of us. Now let's start looking. It's only going to get colder and more dangerous out here for Jimmy. And I for one am not going to give up so easily, no sir, as long as the good Lord keeps me warm and awake, I'm not giving up hope. That little boy is out there somewhere and he needs our help to get him back to his mommy. So let's get moving and get that little boy home."

With that speech and the coffee finished, everyone was revived, and Josh radioed in that they were back on their search and in what direction they were heading. They walked on in silence, each contemplating a different ending to this story. They had now been searching almost an hour and a half when Tommy noticed something sticking up out of the snow. He ran up to it and pulled it out from under a tree. It was a boot, a little boy's boot. Josh caught up with Tom and recognized it as Tommy's.

It was one of the ones he had just bought for the boy. He quickly radioed the information in and asked them to have the ambulance ready. Then suddenly, Josh heard the slightest of sounds. This drew his attention directly to his right. He stopped and raised his hand for everyone else to stop as well. *Tommy was just about to say what?* Then they all heard the same very weak sound coming from a thick, dense section to their right. All four of them looked at each other. This sound was different they had not heard anything like it all night. Quietly, they stepped in the direction of the sound just in case they heard it again. As they continued walking over fallen trees and overgrown brush, they saw in a clearing where another huge tree had fallen. Suddenly, they heard it again, a faint sound. Only this time, it sounded more like a moan, maybe crying, or both. As they walked further in, they heard it loud and clear as Jimmy tried with all his might one last time to cry out. It was a very weak "Help." The three men and Tommy looked at one another in amazement and quickened their paces. As they came upon Jimmy, they stopped dumbfounded. They couldn't believe their eyes.

Jimmy looked up with a tear-stained face, smiled, and said weakly, "Hi, look," pointing to his right. "He's been with me the whole time. Don't be afraid." Just then, a beautiful six-pointed buck stood up and locked his gaze on Josh. Josh raised his hand and smiled at the deer. As the other three looked on in amazement, the deer turned slowly and darted away. Josh as if waking from a trance clapped his hands and started walking toward Jimmy with the others following close behind.

"How ya doing, buddy?" Flynn asked when he reached Jimmy's side.

"I'm okay," Jimmy said in a tired voice.

"Good." Flynn smiled at the boy and said, "how about if we lift this log off, Jimmy, and bring this boy home to his mama?" While this was going on, Sean had radioed in that they had found Jimmy and they should send the paramedics to their location. Tommy was heading in the direction of the opening before the dense area the men had turned into to find this clearing so the paramedics could get Jimmy out.

"So, Jimmy, are you cold?" Sean asked.

"A little, but the deer stayed here with me the whole time, and my new clothes really helped keep me warm. Except I lost one of my boots when I ran away from a tree that was about to fall. But I think if I didn't have the rest of my winter stuff, I probably would've froze to death.

"Josh I prayed that my guardian angel would protect me. Do you think that maybe the deer was him?" Jimmy said weakly but with a touch of excitement.

"I'm almost certain," Josh said with a smile. Josh, Sean, and Flynn huddled together to assess the situation. Jimmy was caught under a large tree that appeared to have fallen across his legs. Josh asked Sean, "Do you think we can lift this tree enough to have Flynn pull Jimmy out from under it or should we try and to lift the tree completely and push it aside and leave Jimmy where he is?" Sean thought for a minute or two surveying the situation and decided. "I know that all first aid lessons tell you to leave the victim where he is until the paramedics arrive. However, in this case, I don't see us being able to physically lift and move that tree completely. So that said, I think we're going to have to lift the tree and have Flynn pull him out from under it." The three men agreed and walked over to Jimmy.

Flynn knelt down next to Jimmy and slowly explained, "Jimmy, Josh and Sean are going to lift this tree off your legs while I pull you out from under it. This might hurt a little when we lift it off, so don't be afraid to yell, okay?"

"Okay," Jimmy said.

"When I count to 3, Josh, you lift the tree with me, and Flynn you pull Jimmy out from under it. Ready, 1, 2, and 3, lift! Now, Flynn, pull Jimmy."

"I got him!" Flynn exclaimed.

"Ugh!" yelled Jimmy. Sean and Josh dropped the tree and ran over to Jimmy and Flynn. Sean took his coat off and put it around Jimmy for extra warmth while they waited for the paramedics. Flynn went to find four strong limbs to use as splints for Jimmy's legs, and Josh held Jimmy's upper body for added warmth.

⚬

It took the paramedics about thirty minutes to get to where Jimmy and the search party were waiting. They had to leave the ambulance back at the diner and walk in with their medical bags and a stretcher.

As the paramedics checked Jimmy out, his mother cried and held him as close as she could. Josh raised his eyes to the evening sky and prayed,

Thank you, Father, for the safety of this child, your child. Thank you for the guidance of the Holy Spirit in our search this evening. Thank you for the protection of your angels that kept Jimmy safe and warm until we were able to return him to his mother here on earth. You are truly amazing and loving. Amen."

Everyone standing echoed his praise and said amen.

It started to snow very softly again so the paramedics quickened their work put Jimmy on the stretcher and began to leave with Maggie standing close next to her son and holding his hand. As the rest of the search and rescue group began to leave, they saw someone walking toward them. Maggie stopped and squinted as she tried to see past the snow that was starting to pick up again. It was hard to make out who it was at first, but suddenly Maggie screamed and ran toward the figure. Jimmy tried to sit up to see who it was, but he was too tired and slumped back down on the stretcher. The man started laughing, picked her up, and swung her around in the air. Then set her down gently and kissed her affectionately. Everyone around Jimmy became excited and happy. Jimmy tried again to sit up and asked.

"Hey what's going on? What happened to my mom? Why did she scream and run away like that?" Suddenly, Jimmy knew the answer. His father was standing next to him and smiling down at him.

"Dad? Dad, is that really you"?

"It sure is, sport! It was supposed to be a surprise tomorrow on Thanksgiving, but when I got to the base, they told me that you had gotten yourself lost, and everyone was out looking for you. I had to come and make sure everything was all right. No one could keep me away. You had everybody scared half to death. When I got to the diner, Jenny told me they found you and that you were all up here and that you were all right maybe a couple of broken legs but basically okay. I thought I had to see for myself. I also figured this was as good a time as any to surprise you both. *Surprise!*"

"I'm sure glad you did, Sad."

"Me too." Maggie echoed as tears flowed uncontrollably down her cheeks. The paramedics reminded everyone that the weather wasn't going to stay on their side much longer so they'd better get moving before a search team would be sent out for all of them. Everyone chuckled, agreed, and started heading out of the clearing and down to the diner. As they walked through the woods, the air seemed electric with energy. Everyone was talking and laughing. Only Flynn turned to Joshua and said with a serious but relaxed face, "Boy we really are lucky."

"What do you mean?" Josh stopped and looked at Flynn with concern.

"What do you mean lucky?"

"Well," Flynn continued, "I mean this scenario could just as easily have gone in a different direction." Josh thought for a moment.

"Yes, I suppose it could have, but I don't think luck had anything to do with it."

"No?" questioned Flynn. "No." Josh shook his head.

"Then how would you explain this?" Flynn asked. At this, Sean and Tommy who were walking just ahead a few steps, heard Flynn's question and stopped and turned to listen to what Josh had to say.

"I know that this area was already checked by another group before us, right?" Flynn and the others nodded. "And they came back saying they found nothing." The others nodded again. "I don't believe in coincidences and luck. I like to believe that, that's when God our Father presents us with a miracle and would like to remain anonymous." As he said that, he smiled and watched to see if the others understood what he meant. Flynn smiled and nodded.

Tommy said, "Oh I get it. Even though Jimmy was lost, God knew we would find him and so…maybe we were kind'ave guided here. Hey! Maybe that deer that was with Jimmy was like a guardian sent by God or something. What do you think, Josh, do you think that might be why that big deer?"

"Stag," Flynn corrected playfully.

"Sorry, was standing there and stayed there the whole time keeping Jimmy warm."

"I think that is a huge possibility."

Sean just stood there staring silently trying to figure this out and finally said, "Well, I don't know, but if we stay out here much longer, we'll be the lost ones." All four guys started to laugh and started to walk quickly down through the woods tracing their steps out to the clearing back to the diner. They watched as they lifted Jimmy into the ambulance and as Maggie and Drew climbed in beside their son. Then Maggie, Drew, Jimmy, and the paramedics drove slowly off to the hospital with an escort by the sheriff's police patrol officer Pat Shepherd.

Most of the searchers stayed and helped at the diner to pitch in and help Jenny and Amber clean up and put it back to its original state. Kate and her husband finished up the dishes and gave hugs all around with an assurance that they would see them Thanksgiving morning at the Annual Community Harvest. Ginger kissed her sad-looking husband, George, good night. *They'd only slept apart a few times in their married lifetime, and he'd hated it.* She told him she loved him, and she'd be home before he even missed her. Then she waved good-bye as the five men—Josh, Flynn, Sean, Tommy, and his dad, Andy, backed out of the parking lot. Then she turned, walked into the diner, put her coat on, and took a sleeping little Ally from Amber's arms. Jenny turned off the lights, locked the doors behind them, and drove Amber home and Ginger and Ally to Maggie and Drew's little house. Jenny came inside and waited while Ginger put Ally down in her bed. Before she turned off the light, she turned on her night light and stole one more peek at her adorable little Ally. When she came downstairs, Ginger offered Jenny some decaf coffee or herbal tea, and Jenny politely said tea would be just wonderful. Ginger fixed coffee for herself and tea for Jenny and fixed a plate of cookies and set everything on the table. Jenny was so complimentary that Ginger blushed.

"Well, sweetie, this isn't much, and besides, it isn't even mine. She giggled.

"I know," Jenny said in a whisper, "but you have no idea how nice it is to have someone fix something for you for a change." Ginger just stared at her for a moment.

"You know, darlin', I never even thought about that. We need one day, and I mean one day real soon, we are going to have a special Jenny day!"

"No." Jenny smiled and shook her head. "You don't have to do that. It's just nice you know."

"Well, sure I know! And don't tell *me* no. I know that I don't have to do anything. But when I set my mind to something, there isn't anyone that is going to change it. Now when is your next day off? We need to make it special. Oh I can't wait."

"Oh all right, if you're certain, then I'll check my calendar and get back to you. I think we should wait until after the holidays though, don't you think?"

"No, I *do* not think. I think you need some TLC now. Now you check that calendar of yours and see how next week looks. Oh, girl, we are going to have some fun." So the two women continued to talk and plan for another hour, and then Jenny decided that since she needed to open the diner early, she better get home and get a good night's sleep. She and Ginger hugged, and Ginger watched as Jenny drove off toward her home.

After dropping the men of Flynn's off, Tommy and his dad drove around to see if anyone still needed any snow plowing. Everyone else went in their own directions to warm up and get some well deserved sleep.

Inside, Flynn turned to George, Sean, and Josh and, smiling at them, said, "That was eventful. Sure am glad you all had such good hearing out there. I'm not so sure I would have heard that little guy's cry, what with my hearing and all. And what a surprise to see Drew! Who would have thought?"

"How long has he been overseas?" Sean inquired. Flynn rubbed his chin and looked at George.

George thought for a moment and said, "I think for at least nine months this time." Josh stopped and looked at George and Flynn and asked, *"This time?"*

"Yep, our boy Drew has already done one tour of duty, and he's on his second tour. He came home this time on leave for only two weeks. He was supposed to have a parade and a motorcycle motorcade with Father Phil and his motorcycle crew on Thanksgiving, but Pat told me with Jimmy missing and he not wanting to be patient, well the surprise really didn't seem as important as saving his son."

Sean looked at Flynn and shook his head and said, "Well, I don't know about any of you, but tonight was quite an eye opener for me. I really wasn't sure we were going to find that little guy. The further we went, the less confident I became. The way the weather was the cold and the darkness. But you were all so levelheaded, so calm. You all had so much faith. I just don't know where that comes from."

George broke in, "Well, you all were lucky to be outside. Being in that diner with Maggie crying and worrying was tough. She really thought there was no hope. She kept blaming herself, kept saying if only she had kept a better eye on him. If only this and if only that. It was a regular cry fest in there."

Josh just looked at the three men, rubbed his hand through his hair, and said, "Faith, you have to have faith that our father had a plan and was looking over us." Sean looked at Josh.

"I know you say that and I know that *you* believe that. It's weird I don't know you hardly at all, but I do know *that* about you. What I don't know is *why*. And I don't know why I find it so hard to believe even a little like you do?"

"Sean, here is something for you to think about tonight as you rest. Our father, *your* father, wants you not always to understand his ways but to believe that the outcome is always greater than we could ever imagine."

With that, Sean bolted upright. He stared into Joshua's eyes, and as Josh looked back, Sean felt a warmth and peace as he had never felt before. George and Flynn walked away and left the two of them that way for only three or four minutes. To Sean, it seemed like thirty. When Josh blinked, Sean slowly closed and opened his eyes. He looked at Josh and asked, "What was that?"

"It's a gift."

"You mean like the one in your handshake?"

"Yes, I guess you could say that. Sean, that was a connection. I know that you have suffered in the past." Sean just nodded; he suddenly felt so tired yet relaxed. "God wants you to know that you are forgiven and that your pain has been taken from you."

"But how do you know that?" Immediately, Sean began to feel stress again.

Josh looked into Sean's eyes and explained, "Sean, it's important for you to give up your past, to be in the present so that when the future arrives, you will be peaceful and calm. Worry and fear only bring more worry and fear. And self-loathing only brings more self-loathing. Look at a bigger picture, Sean, and think of others before you think of yourself. Remember we've been given a guide, the Holy Spirit, that will guide us and continue to give us strength throughout our lifetimes." With that said, he was tired and hoped Sean didn't mind as he hugged him and said good night.

Sean asked if he would mind talking more later.

"I really appreciate this talk. No one has ever really spoken to me with such a spiritual message before."

Josh smiled and said, "Maybe your heart wasn't ready to hear."

"Yeah maybe." Sean lowered his head. "Well, I'll see you tomorrow."

<hr>

Flynn and George were in the kitchen getting things ready for the next morning. Flynn got the coffee set up, and George put the dishes on the cupboard and set the silverware around the table in the dining room. Flynn was glad that he had put the chili and corn bread away earlier so that he wouldn't have to handle that tonight. They could all have that for tomorrow night's dinner. Flynn asked George what he thought about what was going on between Josh and Sean and wondered if Josh was going to help Sean sort a few things out. George shrugged his shoulders and said, "I don't know. Sean is a tough nut to crack. He's been struggling with his faith or lack thereof for quite some time now. I certainly wish him luck."

As Josh headed up the stairs, Sean went into the living room and had a glass of brandy that sat on the cart in front of the picture window. After filling his glass, he crossed the room and sat on the couch facing the fireplace. He just sat there staring the fire as the fire was still smoldering. Flynn still in the kitchen began to turn off lights and unplugged the electrical appliances checking once again that he had everything in order for tomorrow.

George went to the telephone room to call the love of his life and knew that Ginger was in her element taking care of that little darling Ally. She loved children. It was a shame that they had never been blessed with children of their own; however, that only made him love her all the more. She was every child's grandma here in Munising, and she wouldn't have it any other way.

The children of Munising had given her more joy than if she had had ten of her own. She was special that was for sure. He sure was glad the she was his. He doesn't know what he'd do without her. George and Ginger had been married for forty years. He couldn't think of one argument or hurtful word that ever crossed their threshold. He loved *his spicy* redhead, and that was just the way it was. Every time she smiled at him, his stomach still did flip-flap. *Now that's something*, he thought. They never went to bed without saying I love you, and tonight won't be an exception.

Just as he hung up, Flynn popped his head in and said goodnight to everyone and asked if George wouldn't mind locking up. "Nope, sounds great, but what about Ms. Beam, do you know if she is home yet?" asked George.

Flynn yelled over his shoulder, "Yep, saw her car in the drive. She must have come home during that small break in the storm. Everyone's in and cozy for the night. I'll head on over to the little house and see y'all in the morning at breakfast. Goodnight, George, good night, Sean." George nodded. Sean quietly said good night to the men and said, "I'll go up in a few."

Josh was all washed up and sitting on the edge of his bed, writing the events of the day in his journal.

Today certainly was an interesting day for me, Father. Your unending love and the security of your faithfulness to your children here does, at times, seem to go unnoticed. This saddens me and shows me that the plan of yours for me to come again at this time is needed. The people here in Munising do need me and need you. With the Holy Spirit's guidance, I will be able to do your will without the people of the town ever knowing my identity. Again, I thank you for your kindness and guidance in finding Jimmy. Thanksgiving will take on a new meaning this year for Munising. I thank you for your graces in all our yesterdays, todays, and tomorrows that have yet to come. Amen.

Josh climbed into bed. He felt that he had had a full day. As he closed his eyes, he could only imagine what the next few days would bring. He knew that whatever it was, it would be full of excitement, and he was looking forward to it with welcoming hands.

Downstairs, Sean got up off the sofa and walked over to the window and began a long litany in his head as he watched the snow plows work their magic on the roads and as the late-night drivers slowly crept their way home as the storm slowly came to a stop. He couldn't get over the fact that he was so willing to give up on finding Jimmy. It really was so early in their search.

Why had I not had the faith or the courage to continue the way Flynn, Josh, and Tommy had? Tommy, even Tommy, had more faith. Man, what's wrong with me? Maybe if I could just believe in something, I don't know, anything, maybe I would have felt different. And what about this Josh guy? Seems like he prays a lot! He's not pushy though. That's good. That conversation sure was interesting, his eyes, and that handshake too. I don't know. I think that there is something in what he has to say. I just, oh, maybe if we get a chance to talk some more. And how come no one said anything about what happened with the deer and him? Was I the only one that saw that? What was that all about? Oh well, the little guy was found and he seems okay.

He shook the thoughts from his head and took his glass into the kitchen. Then Sean locked the doors went upstairs, washed up, and went straight to bed. He had a hard time sleeping that night. The picture of the deer and Josh looking at each other in a trancelike state just wouldn't leave his memory.

In the meantime, Flynn was in his little house sitting in his favorite chair in front of a nice, warm fire, sipping a warm cup of cocoa. He too was thinking about the occurrences of the evening.

Wasn't it wonderful that we were able to find that little guy? Imagine that deer staying by his side the whole time protecting him and keeping him warm and his father coming home from Afghanistan. Now that will be a news story for the Munising Weekly that's for sure, he thought as he smiled to himself. *The only thing that was strange was that that deer acted like he knew Josh or something. Odd, I have to admit. Almost like they were old friends the way they looked at each other. He sure does a lot of praying and that reaction you get when you shake his hand. I wonder if that happens to anyone else. Maybe I'll ask Harry. I'm sure they shook hands. I know a lot of praying people, but well what, does it matter a little extra prayer doesn't hurt anyone*, he thought. *He certainly is friendly and ready to help. Who am I to judge people?*

He queried as he got himself up and ready for bed.

In bed, Flynn found himself thanking God for his help and asking him to look out for his dear wife as he fell sound asleep.

Chapter 13

Getting Ready

The next morning was a brand-new day. The sun was shining. The sky was the brightest winter blue sky imaginable. The snow sparkled as if diamonds had been cast by God himself while the world slept. It was the most beautiful morning. It did not go unnoticed either. Josh jumped out of bed, washed, and readied himself for the day. On his way down the stairs, he ran into Sean and Ms. Beam as they all commented on the beautiful morning. When they got to the dining room, they noticed that George and Ginger were just starting their coffee while Tom was bringing them their breakfasts.

"Umm, that looks terrific," commented Josh. "What is that?"

"This is Flynn's famous stuffed French toast," said Tommy. "If you have this, you won't need anything else for the rest of the day."

"That's for sure," George piped in. "They are really delicious." The three boarders standing in the doorway could only look and nod their heads as they made their way to their seats.

When Tom came to get their orders, each one replied in unison, "I want what they're having."

Tom just smiled and said, "Coming right up." He then showed up with Sean's and Josh's carafes of coffee and a carafe of hot water and Mrs. Earl Grey tea for Ms. Beam.

As they waited, there was some conversation about the night before. Ms. Beam couldn't believe she had missed all the excitement. She realized something was up when she got home and no one was home.

"I tried to stay up and wait for someone to get home, but I just couldn't keep my eyes open anymore. Plus the quick note you left me, Ginger, was thoughtful, at least I knew you were all safe."

Josh asked, "Ginger, when did you get back, late last night or early this morning?"

"Drew dropped me off about a half hour ago."

"How is everything at the Stone household?" Sean asked.

"Well, as you can imagine, a little shaken. Maggie is still at the hospital with Jimmy. He has two broken legs."

"Two broken legs, my word," interjected Ms. Beam.

"Yes, and he'll be at the hospital for a little while. Jenny is going to take care of Ally tomorrow during the Vet's Thanksgiving Feast, and then they're all going to the hospital to have Thanksgiving with Jimmy. So they won't be sharing with us after the feast. Maggie wanted me to let you know that, Ms. Beam, for the head count." Ms. Beam nodded and poured herself some tea.

"What's this about a Vet's Thanksgiving Feast?" Sean inquired about the Munising Annual Veteran's Thanksgiving Feast. Both Sean and Josh were newcomers, so this caught their attention, and they started asking for some specifics. Their questions were a little overwhelming to Ms. Beam, so Ginger smiled at her and, with her usual flair, took over.

"Do either of you know about the Annual Community Harvest?" The two looked at each other with interest and shrugged their shoulders and looked back at Ginger eagerly, willing her to continue.

"The harvest itself will be held tomorrow morning. It starts bright and early, around 7:00. It ends around 12:00 p.m. It's put on every year by the local Jaycee chapter, Chamber of Commerce, and our Local Food Pantry. People from the community donate all kinds of nonperishable foods and other items to help out our not so fortunate people and families of our community," Ginger explained.

"We also have a special collection for coffee, tea, breath mints, store-bought cookies, candy, and paperback books for the men and women overseas. The Veterans handle that end of it," George continued.

"Actually, I believe it was our Maggie Stone and Kate from the Novel-Tea that started that up with the Vets, wasn't it, Ginger?"

"Yes, it was," Ginger confirmed.

Sean and Josh together asked, "How can we help?"

"I'm sure if you show up at the junior high school on Main Street they'll find plenty for you to do," Ms. Beam said smiling shyly.

Josh and Sean thanked Ms. Beam and Ginger for the info. They both smiled back, and much to Ms. Beam's chagrin her cheeks turned slightly pink out of embarrassment. Ginger just smiled and waved their politeness off.

After eating breakfast and complimenting the chef, Josh asked Flynn if there was anything he could do to help him out since he wasn't scheduled to work just yet.

Flynn smiled and handed him a dish towel.

"Hope you know what to do with this."

"I sure do. My mom taught me at a very young age." Josh smiled as he took a wet dish from Flynn. They chatted happily as they quickly worked through the kitchen chores.

With the kitchen work finished, Flynn disappeared through the mudroom and came back carrying one of the biggest frozen turkeys Josh had ever seen.

"Wow! Where in the world and who in the world is going to eat all that turkey?" Josh asked in amazement.

"Well"—Flynn smiled—"this turkey is for the Annual Veteran's Thanksgiving Feast held right here in Flynn's Boarding House."

"Really?" Josh asked.

"Really," Flynn said. It started off as a little dinner when Alice was still here. We invited just a few people and one of the armed servicemen or women from the local base. These men and or women can't get home, so we thought, well, we could at least feed one of them for Thanksgiving. Well, the second year, the officer we fed the year before wondered if he could bring one his fellow officers with him. He said he'd even pay for himself. Of course we said yes, and no way was he going to pay for it. After that Thanksgiving, Alice and I decided we'd just invite the whole crew of them over the next year and see if maybe some of the townsfolk would help us out with the fixings and the serving. Sure enough they were jumping at the chance.

"That's when Maggie and Kate decided to collect coffee, tea, breath mints, and paperbacks. We give them to the officers, and they get them shipped out. It's a match made in heaven."

"It is that, my friend. It certainly is that," Josh said as he stole a quick look heavenward. "How can I help?" He asked.

"I thought you'd never ask." Flynn grinned.

Well, downstairs are the tables and chairs. We can start there." Josh brought the tables and chairs up from downstairs; he began to set them up in the living room. Sean and George had already rearranged the furniture so that there was plenty of open space. Ginger was ironing the table cloths, and Ms. Beam was making small center pieces for the tables and putting silverware and napkins together for the table settings. Everyone from the boarding house was busy working inside. Tommy and his father were outside clearing the driveway and the sidewalks of the snow that had fallen the day before.

Several tables were soon set up in the living room with gold and rust-colored tablecloths. Each table had a beautiful centerpiece of silk mums in cream and burgundy with gold and green leaves surrounding short gold-colored candles. The table settings had vintage china of Franciscan apple with cream-colored napkins wrapped around the silverware. All of this was set up perfectly around the fireplace and made the room look warm and inviting. When Ginger and Ms. Beam were satisfied with their work and the ambiance of the room, they smiled and headed to the dining room.

Here they placed a gold tablecloth with a sheer light-burgundy overlay on top of the large dining table that was centered in the middle of the room. Then they placed two larger centerpieces that matched the ones on the tables that were in the living room, on the center of the table. Here, however, the candles were taller and cream-colored instead of gold. On this table, they would place all the food, banquet-style, that all the townspeople will be bringing for the feast, with the turkey at the head of the table.

———

Flynn walked into the living room and then into the dining room and gave a low whistle of admiration. Both women looked up and blushed. Flynn stood there and said, "Wow, you two sure know how to transform a room, don't you? Sean, Josh, George, come in here checkout what these two very talented ladies have been doing all afternoon."

"Well, I'll be," said George. "This doesn't look like the same place, does it, boys?"

"No, sir" Josh and Sean said in unison. At that, all four of them started applauding and whistling. The two ladies blushed and curtsied playing into their little bit of fun.

Chapter 14

Diner, Dinner

After all that hoot'n and holler'n, Sean noticed that they had been working well into the late afternoon. He suggested that they all go over to the diner for a bite to eat. "Everyone fore say yea, anyone against say nay." Everyone raised their hands and, in unison, said yea.

Flynn suddenly thought about the chili and cornbread he had made the day before. Then he had an idea. He decided to bring it over to Tommy's house to give his mom a night off. She had always loved his chili and thought this would also be one way of being neighborly, especially after all the work Tommy and Andy did on the driveway and walks today. As the group got ready to go, Flynn grabbed everything out of the fridge, grabbed his jacket from the mudroom, and headed over to Tommy's. He knocked on the door, and Sarah, Andy's wife, answered the door. Sarah was a beautiful woman with dark-brown hair, warm brown eyes, and a smile that lit up a room.

"Flynn, come in, come in. Well, what do you have there?"

"Hello, Sarah, my, don't you look lovely," Flynn said

"Thank you, what a nice compliment. Did you need Tommy for something?"

"No, no, of course not. Listen I've got some chili and cornbread here. I thought you might like to take a night off of cooking, and the boys have been working up such an appetite all day."

"How sweet, Flynn, thank you so much. The boys and I will really enjoy this. You know how much I love your chili. You didn't have to do this you know."

"I know I didn't. You all just enjoy. We'll see you at the Harvest tomorrow, right?"

"Yes, you will. Thanks again, Flynn. You're an angel." Both Sarah and Flynn hugged and said good night as he walked out the door.

When Flynn crossed over to his driveway, all his boarders were waiting for him. George, Ginger, and Ms. Beam jumped into their little bug and said they'd meet the rest of them at Jenny's. Sean, Josh, and Flynn got into Flynn's Range Rover and followed them out the drive. Soon they were all sitting comfortably in a booth at Jenny's when Amber came over and flashed her bright and cheerful smile.

"Well, what have we here?" she asked.

Flynn of course smiled and said, "You, young lady, have six very hungry customers. What's the special for the day?"

"Tonight our special is Cobb salad with crispy chicken and your choice of onion soup or vegetable soup and a fresh baked roll. We figured that a lot of people wouldn't want a big meal today because of tomorrow."

"That makes sense," said Josh.

"I think I'll have the special," said Ginger. Josh, Florence, and Flynn agreed; Sean had a hot beef plate, and George asked for a hamburger and fries.

"That's right," Ginger said, "go ahead and order yourself up a heart attack right here right now. That's just what we need after yesterday's excitement."

"Now, Ginger, c'mon once in a while won't hurt me. Right?"

"Oh all right, I guess you worked pretty hard today you deserve a burger," she said as she patted his hand.

While they waited for their food, Josh asked an unusual question. So he started a bit timidly. "You all know that this is my first time in the States during this time of year." The group looked at him and nodded yes. "Well," he continued, "it's also the first time that I've ever really heard about Thanksgiving. At this, Sean's jaw dropped. George almost spit his coffee out right there and then. Ms. Beam's and Flynn's eyes almost bugged out of their heads. And Ginger just stared and shook her head and of course was the first one to speak. "You poor child, really you've never heard of Thanksgiving?"

"No, ma'am. I have not."

"Well, here comes one, of many, I'm sure, history lessons. Many years ago when America was discovered and when the British came here, it was considered the new land then. These people traveled all the way from Europe. You will like this part. They came here mostly for religious freedoms. A lot of people were being persecuted in Europe because they didn't believe in the same religion that their king and queen did. So they decided to come over here. After many months on a boat crossing the ocean and many people dying during their journey, they finally made it here. What they didn't count on was the fact that the soil and animals and climate would be so different. That first winter here, they lost more people. They were just about to give up when they met the Native American Indians. The Native Americans taught these people how to hunt these new animals. They also taught them how to cook their meat and use their fur for warmth. The Indians taught them what vegetables grow in this climate and how to harvest and prepare them." Josh sat there listening, amazed at the hospitality that the Indians showed. "Anyway," Ginger concluded, "the pilgrims showed the Indians also many things that helped the Indians to progress. Long story short, Thanksgiving is the first day that the Indians and the pilgrims sat down together and gave thanks for their bountiful harvest. They then shared a fantastic meal together."

"It's held in November because the farmers harvest all their grain and produce at that time," Flynn said."

"Wow, that's quite a story," Josh said looking at his friends. It's such a simple thing to do, but it carries such a tremendous meaning—giving thanks." As they were all agreeing, Amber brought out their food, and as they passed their plates, Amber asked if they had heard anymore on Jimmy. Ginger said she had gotten home around 7:30 that morning. When Drew came home to relieve her, he said, "They weren't going to release Jimmy for a while yet and that he and Ally would relieve Maggie after lunch so that she could get cleaned up and pack a few things to stay with him for the next few days. Ginger said that Maggie was still in shock over all the excitement and the surprise of Drew being home."

"He has two broken legs. It's a miracle that he didn't have frostbite or worse being exposed to the cold for that length of time," Amber said in amazement.

Sean, still remembering the event, said, "Yeah, but if you'd seen the stag that was resting near him keeping him warm, well…"

"I know," Flynn chimed in.

"He was a six pointer. Can you imagine? Why that little boy must have been so scared at first."

"Those animals are so big up close," commented Florence.

"It sure was something." Josh smiled to himself

"I wonder if Maggie will be able to help tomorrow," Amber questioned. Then Ginger explained that Jenny was going to take care of Ally and that Maggie's mamma and dad were going to stay with Jimmy during the Veteran's Feast. Maggie said that she and Drew had planned to be at Kate's and Mac's early enough to help bring the books to the feast and help out there. They won't be able to stay and have our little Thanksgiving after though. That's when they plan on going back to the hospital to have a very special Thanksgiving with Jimmy. They were going to Flynn's together so there was no need to worry. They have everything under control.

The group continued with their meals and light conversation until Amber brought the bill. Flynn snatched it and said with a stern voice, "There's no use arguing. I've got this. Here you go, Amber. Now go ahead and keep the change. We'll see you tomorrow at the Harvest, won't we?"

"You bet you will, Mr. McNamee. Thanks for the tip," Amber said as she turned to walk toward the cash register.

When dinner was finished and with bill all settled, they all headed back to the boarding house to relax before the big day tomorrow. In the driveway of the boarding house, Ms. Beam bid everyone good night and went straight to her room. Ginger, George, Flynn, and Sean decided to play a game of scrabble in the kitchen. Josh decided to take a short walk and said that he would join them for the next game.

Chapter 15

Meeting Father Phil

Josh watched as his newfound friends stepped away from the car into the house. While outside, Josh breathed in the fresh, cold air, smiled to himself as he put his hat on, and shoved his hands into his parka pockets. He decided to walk straight and cross the highway. It was deserted and quiet, and the stillness made him think of a place he'd like to be right now. So off he headed to St. Mathew's the Catholic church a few short blocks from where he was standing. As he walked, he saw many houses that were closed up tight against the elements and the possible dangers that plague the thoughts of this tiny community. He thought in the last few days he hadn't really had much time to listen to the news on the television or radio. He had, however, read a bit in the newspaper and heard some pieces of information from the townsfolk.

Times had changed a great deal since his last visit that he barely recognized the world anymore. So much technology, so many more material things, the medical sciences had improved leaps and bounds. But people interestingly hadn't changed all that much. You still had the few that in so many ways wanted to do what's right and to help those that are in need, but they just don't know where to begin or don't think that their effort alone is enough to really do anything.

So far, Josh was astounded that here in Munising, the community seemed to be looking out for one another. As he reached St. Matt's, he pondered on that for a few minutes and shook his head with a feeling of gratitude filling his heart.

Climbing the stairs, Josh felt his heart quicken with anticipation knowing that he would be able to enter his house and spend time in meditation and prayer with his father. He grabbed the handle and pulled. To his surprise, he found that the door wouldn't open. He tried again. Again the door wouldn't budge. Just as he let go of the door, Father Phil startled him, asking, "May I help you?"

Josh turned and said, "Uh, yes, I was trying to go inside for a private moment with the father, and for some reason, someone has mistakenly locked the doors."

"I'm sorry. I'm Father Phil," he said extending his hand.

"I'm Josh," Josh replied taking his hand in his.

"It's nice to meet you." As Father Phil's and Josh's hands held, Father Phil's breath was taken and he was filled with a feeling of wonderment. He looked at Josh; Josh smiled at him and slowly released his hand. As Father Phil let go, he looked at his hand and then back at Josh and smiled as he grabbed his hand with his other hand.

When he caught his breath, he asked, "What *was* that?"

"That? That's just something that happens sometimes when I meet very important people. Now back to the doors, why are they locked?" he asked shifting his weight.

"Unfortunately, it's no mistake," Father Phil started to explain. "We lock the doors around 6:30 p.m. each night, except holy days when we have mass in the evenings. You must be new in this community."

"Yes, I am. I'm staying at Flynn's Boarding House," Josh explained

"Flynn's, well you've got the best place in town. He'll take good care of you there."

"So why, if you don't mind my asking, do you lock the church's doors?"

"Way back about five maybe six years ago, we used to keep the doors open and have some parishioners walk in and out to be our security. Unfortunately, one night when we were between security checks, someone came in and broke several statues, turned over our vigil light stand, and stole some sacred things from sacristy." Josh couldn't believe what he was hearing. He asked if anything was recovered.

"No," Father Phil said sadly.

He also said, "Unfortunately, there has been a rash of them again this year just as other churches were beginning to feel it was safe to open their doors again."

"Isn't there any way that we can prevent this?" Josh asked.

"We could put in security cameras and have volunteers on the hour, but that is very expensive and timely, and we are in poor economic times right now," Father explained.

"Yes, I guess I can understand, but having more time to pray and share their faith wouldn't that help the people through? I mean, isn't this when people really need a place to go, to really feel a connection with their Master?" Josh said with a quiet passion.

"I feel as you do, but right now, my hands are tied." Father Phil hung his head sadly.

"Would you be open to talk to me more about this, Father, at a more pleasant and warmer situation?" Josh asked and looked around as he smiled warmly. I might have some ideas that may be of some help to you and some of the other church leaders. I know that I'm new to the area, but I would really like to help out *if* you would be interested."

"Interested, absolutely, Josh, come by any time. My quarters are connected to the church. I have an open-door policy. I would be happy and grateful to listen to your ideas. Maybe I could invite some of the other church leaders as well, would that be all right?"

"Absolutely, the more, the merrier," Josh said smiling.

"It was very nice to meet you," Father Phil said warmly.

"Nice meeting you as well, and have a blessed Thanksgiving," Josh responded as both men shook hands again and parted.

***

As Josh walked away, Father Phil looked at his hand still feeling the extreme warmth that spread from Josh's hand to his like the warmth you feel as your hand is slowly immersed in warm water.

He walked solemnly back to the rectory feeling this same warmth spread to his heart and end with a smile on his face.

By the time Josh had made it home, his housemates had gone off to bed and left him a note.

Josh,

Sorry we finished our game and just couldn't keep our eyes open any longer. Ginger still remains the reigning Scrabble Queen! See you bright and early if you plan on coming to the Harvest in the morning. Wake up call is 7:00 a.m.

Good night, Flynn
PS

Cookies on the counter, milk in the fridge.

Josh smiled to himself as he walked to the kitchen counter and found three cookies wrapped on a plate. He grabbed one and rewrapped the rest and headed up the stairs for a contemplative sleep.

Chapter 16

The Sowing of the Harvest

The next morning, Josh woke with a start as he heard soft knocking on his door and the familiar voice of Flynn greeting him with a pleasant, "Happy Thanksgiving, Josh." Josh smiled and returned the greeting as he lifted himself out of bed.

He opened his door and asked.

"How much time do I have before we leave for the Harvest?"

Flynn answered jovially, "We have about thirty minutes. First we have to go around in Andy's truck from next door and pick up some of the neighbor's bags of goods that they can't deliver themselves. If you don't want to help with that, then you have about one and a half hours."

Josh rubbed his eyes and said, "Give me ten minutes, and I'll be in the foyer ready to go."

"Okay,"—Flynn nodded—"I'll rustle the others and get everyone's coffee ready. Remember you'll find it in the kitchen because the dining area is set up for the Veteran's Feast later."

"You bet!" Josh exclaimed "I'll be right down." Josh said a quick prayer praising his father for the kindness of all the people today working so hard to provide for others not so bountiful. He then asked that all the events and festivities run smoothly and that cooperation is the way of the day. As he was blessing himself he was quickly reminded of Father Phil and hoped he would be blessed to see him today.

He rose off the floor, grabbed his shoes, and headed down the stairs stopping only a moment once again to take in the view from the landing window. Lake Superior was wild today. Her waves were crashing roughly against the shore. This gave him the feeling that he didn't dress quite warm enough. He ran back up stairs to his room and pulled his sweater off, put a turtle neck shirt on and then the sweater again. After, Josh could only sigh with satisfaction. As he turned, he noticed Ms. Beam going into the washroom and asked if she was going with them over to the Harvest.

She shook her head no and said, "No, I don't really do the Harvest. I usually stay behind to watch the turkey which Flynn is getting ready on the grill. I might pop over just to say hello, but my role is here today." She waved good-bye, and Josh continued down the stairs.

Once downstairs, he walked into the kitchen where he ran into Sean, Ginger, and George already fixing their cups of coffee and grabbing a donut that Flynn had generously laid out for them.

"Happy Thanksgiving" they said in unison. He smiled and replied with the same greeting.

"Got your muscles warmed up" Ginger inquired?

"I guess" Josh answered questioningly.

"Oh, don't mind her" George laughed. "She's just teasing. She knows that there is a lot of lifting and bending at the Harvest is all. Did you get a good night sleep?"

"I did actually although I did run into Father Phil last night at St. Matt's."

"At the church?" Ginger asked. "What on earth were you doing at the church at that hour and what was Father Phil doing out and about at that hour?"

"First," Josh said, "I was walking and thought I would check out St. Matt's and found that the doors were locked. As I was standing there, Father Phil was out doing a quick check on the church. So we ended up having a very interesting conversation about what's been happening to the churches and what happened in the past to his church."

"Sad really," George said under his breath.

"Sad?" Ginger said indignantly. "Sad my rear end. It is absolutely unthinkable that anybody would go into a place of God and do the kind of destructive things that they had done. It's a sorry society if you ask me. To think that our country is in the economic situation it's in and they start attacking our holy places. They know we can't afford to fix them or replace what they have ruined. It's disgraceful if you ask me."

The room was very quiet after that. Josh was surprised at the passion that he saw in Ginger. However, it gave him hope that maybe, just maybe, she isn't the only one, at least, in this community that would be willing to do something to make some changes, some big changes.

"Well, after we talked a bit, I asked if maybe we could get together with some of the other church leaders and come up with some solutions to problems they've all been having." Ginger and George seemed very interested and offered their support if he needed any.

Just then, Flynn walked in and looked at his boarders and, with just a hint of pride, thought, *This is exactly what Alice had in mind when she thought of our little boarding house. I'm sure of it.*

Rubbing his hands together, he told them, "The bird is all set and cooking as I speak."

"Okay, here's the plan. I'll drop George and Ginger off at the site and get the list of pickups. Then I'll come back for you and Josh," Flynn explained as he pointed to Sean and Josh. Then we'll go around town and get all of those bags and boxes of donations. Does that sound all right to you two?" Josh and Sean nodded in unison as they took bites of their donuts.

"Good c'mon, folks, let's get going. People are waiting for us." Ginger and George grabbed their travel mugs and coats and followed Flynn out the back door. Sean and Josh finished eating and filled their mugs with coffee. Then they began cleaning up the kitchen so that it wouldn't be an issue when they got back. They left the remaining donuts and the carafe of hot water and the tea bags on the table for Ms. Beam. When they finished, Flynn was back. Grabbing their jackets and the coffee mugs, the two of them ran out the door to start their Thanksgiving Day.

Ms. Beam waited until she heard the door shut and then entered the kitchen and looked around. She smiled when she saw that they had been so thoughtful to leave her some donuts and the tea. She really isn't very good with crowds. *Yesterday was a little more than I usually take,* she thought. *I know they mean well. It's just I so like my privacy. I enjoy their company, and I enjoy helping. I just need to have my space.* She resigned to herself. After her little breakfast, she carefully wrapped the last donut put away the teas, and wiped down the table. She looked around, and when she was satisfied with the cleanliness of the kitchen, she grabbed her jacket and went outside to check on the turkey.

━━━━━◆━━━━━

The turkey looked beautiful. It was cooking up a nice golden brown and smelled delicious; although, she couldn't understand why in the world anyone would possibly want to cook a turkey outside on a grill in November. She just didn't understand it. Well, her job was to check on it and to set the tables, and that was exactly what she was going to do. She was not going to fall down at her post.

With that thought in mind, she saw Sarah coming over holding her cup of coffee. Florence enjoyed talking with Sarah; actually, she enjoyed Sarah's company altogether. Then again, she thought everyone enjoyed Sarah's company. There wasn't a bad thing about Sarah. "How's that turkey cooking over there, Flo? Sarah asked as she crossed the drive to Flynn's backyard. It sure is a big one this year, isn't it?"

"Yes," Ms. Beam answered. "I think we've got about three more soldiers this year than last. You do know how those men and women can eat, don't you?" Both women smiled.

"It sure is sad though," Sarah said.

"What?" Ms. Beam asked.

"Well, all these soldiers being so far away from their families especially this time of year."

"I know. You're right. I thank God that we can at least do this for them. At least give them some sort of feeling of home," Ms. Beam countered.

"I guess so," Sarah quietly agreed. "Well, anyway you look at it, the turkey is checked, and I better get back inside and put some Christmas music on, even if it is a day early."

"Do you need any help setting anything up inside, Flo? I'd really like to help if I could."

"Not too much. I just need to get the china out and start receiving the food from the community. If you'd like to help with that, I'd greatly appreciate it," Ms. Beam said with a smile.

"That would be lovely," Sarah agreed as they both went into the house chatting easily.

First, Ms. Beam went to the dining area, took the good china out of the cabinets, and showed Sarah how she wanted the tables in the living room set. Sarah caught on quickly and got right down to business setting the tables. Ms. Beam started answering the door as a stream of people started to arrive with bowls, platters dishes, hot plates, punch bowls, and coffee carafes.

Chapter 17

The Gathering of Goods

While Flynn drove, Josh and Sean ran up and down the streets and apartment hallways picking up donations for the Harvest. They seemed to be making record time when Flynn realized that the load seemed much less this year than last.

He shook his head as he said, "It sure is sad when so many of the folks that donated at one time are finding themselves as the recipients of the Harvest themselves this year."

"You know I wondered about what Sean mentioned, that some of the people from other houses have stopped me and apologized for not giving this year. They've been giving me all kinds of explanations. It's really hard to believe."

Josh agreed, "The same thing has been happening to me. How long has this been going on?" Flynn and Sean looked at each other in shock.

Then Flynn asked, "Where have you been, Josh? Have you been living under a rock or something?"

"No, I know that the economy is bad and that there are poor, but that it has become so wide spread is my question. When did that happen?"

"Well, if you ask me," Flynn interjected, "I think some of it comes from feeling so hopeless. These here folks have lost Faith. They don't think God is listening."

"How can they think that? The Father listens all the time. He has plans and purposes for everyone here."

"Well, it's easy for you," said Sean. "It's clear that you have a strong sense of your spirituality, but well, take me for instance, I'm just not all that sure."

"Oh," Josh said almost in a whisper. "What makes you feel that you aren't being listened to?"

"I guess times like this, hearing these stories. Sometimes I have to wonder. When so many of our politicians seem to be only after their own interests."

"What exactly does that mean? asked a quizzical Josh. "I thought that with today's technology and so many with riches beyond measure, the poor would be taken better care of. But from what I'm to understand is that the people who are governing are only taking care of themselves, and the less fortunate aren't any better off."

"That's correct," said Josh.

"That's only the half of it. Unfortunately, the United States was the only country that people could go to, to find shelter to find freedom, real freedom," Sean said passionately.

As Josh watched, he said, "So what's changed?"

"What's changed?" Sean and Flynn asked incredulously.

Then Flynn jumped in. "I'll tell you what's changed, our government that's what. They've made all of us, especially our kids, believe that they have no hope, that this government will take care of us and them, well, everything, that the only faith they need is faith in their government to bail them out. What so many people in our country don't understand is that the more the government promises, the more the tax payers will suffer. While the rest of the world watches with bated breath waiting for the greatest country in the world to fall and crumble before their eyes. Something they've been waiting for forever. While we stand and watch everything we worked for and built up be destroyed."

"Here are my questions." Sean asked, "When the young wake up, will it be too late? And what country can we immigrate to, to help and protect us? Nowhere that's where."

Just then Flynn pulled into the site and was greeted by some very eager boy scouts ready to help them unload the truck of its bags and boxes.

Before they all got out of the truck, they all looked at each and smiled as Flynn said, "That is a conversation for another time. Right now, the good old US of A is still the best there is and this is why. We care, and we still have the provisions to help when help is needed." Josh and Sean jumped into the flatbed and started handing out the goods. The boys brought everything to a table where it was then dispersed to their designated areas.

Josh couldn't believe his eyes. The storage site was a warehouse that used to be a carpet store before it moved to another community. It was filled with tables that had laminated signs attached to poles that told people where to bring specific items that were being donated. There were tables for canned vegetables, canned fruit, soup, detergent, diapers, and other nonperishable items. The room was packed with people of all ages.

There were people standing behind the tables filling boxes and others carrying full boxes over to the back area of the warehouse. There were people standing at a check in station taking boxes and bags and handing them to teenagers, toddlers holding their parents hands. In another area were people filling boxes with different items that were marked Share-a-Christmas.

There were beverages and donuts that appeared to have been donated and even Santa was there to entertain the children. Everything looked to be very organized. Josh was amazed at the energy and joyfulness that was electrifying the room and those involved in the project. There had to be over a hundred people of all ages here. Sean stood there in disbelief. Flynn came up behind him and said, "Now this, this warms your heart, doesn't it?" Sean just stood there speechless just staring and nodding his head. He had never seen anything like this before. As he looked around, he saw several of his students there. Some of the students were alone, some with whole families, and some with just younger or older siblings. He took a couple of minutes and spoke with as many as he could to find out what brought them out there this morning. He was amazed by some stories of families that were once recipients and now were doing their best to help others and others that were doing community service with their churches confirmation class.

Josh caught up with Sean awhile later after he himself had talked with several people including children and Father Phil who had introduced him to several of the other religious leaders of the community and said

"Who do you think these people hear? Who do you think they're answering to right now, Sean? They have faith and a belief that because they can, they should. Their faith in God is strong, and because of that, Sean, they know they've been blessed. They're here to share their blessings."

"Look there's Tommy's family," Josh said as he slapped Sean back to consciousness. "This is really amazing," Josh said as he and Sean turned to bring more goods in from other trucks that were arriving steadily throughout the morning.

After all their goods were in, the three men rolled up their sleeves and were given tasks to do. Flynn started to empty boxes and bring their contents to their designated destinations. Sean began directing people as to where their particular items belonged, and Josh went over to the Jaycees and started filling boxes for needy families and their Share-A-Christmas Program. He also helped divide the boxes between the Share-A-Christmas Program and the County's Food Pantry shelves. The Girl Scouts were singing Christmas carols, and the Salvation Army accompanied them on their instruments.

At eleven, everything slowed down, and the men started to break the site down. They stacked the tables and chairs so that by twelve, the site was completely cleared out. My goodness, you'd never know anything so wonderful had just happened not twenty minutes ago, would you," Flynn said finishing his last cup of coffee. Flynn, Josh, and Sean said their good-byes and synchronized their watches with George, Ginger, Kate, Mac, and all the others that were meeting them back at the boarding house. The three men joyfully hopped in the truck and went straight back to the house. George and Ginger were getting a ride with Kate and Mac.

Chapter 18

Thanksgiving Blessings

When they all arrived at the house, they scattered to their rooms to clean up. Kate and Mac went to Ms. Beam's room, which she had arranged with them the week before. Flynn checked on the turkey, and it looked fantastic and was cooking right on schedule. It was a good thing that he didn't have to prepare anything else for the feast. He knew that anything else would be too stressful for him. That done, he went in his little house and changed for his guests, which would be arriving in about three hours.

⁓

Back at the big house, townspeople were arriving with vegetables, hot and cold casseroles, potatoes of every kind, salads, breads, pies, cakes, and cookies. Some brought sodas, milk, and punch. After Kate, Ginger, Ms. Beam, and Sarah finished sorting the foods in hot and cold order. Then they arranged the first course on the table just as Flynn came in beaming with delight. He gave each contributing neighbor a warm hug and sincere thank you. Then he singled out Ms. Beam and took her hands in his and thanked her especially for the extra beautiful table decorations and the table settings. He was very grateful for all her work and extra touches. She smiled and blushed as she took his compliments. Then she turned to Sarah who was quietly standing off to the side and said, "I never would have been able to do it this year without the wonderful help and conversation of Sarah."

Flynn looked up and saw Sarah standing there and walked the short distance across the room and enveloped her in his arms with a big bear hug and said

"Well thank you to you too, Sarah, for helping and for being the best of neighbors." Sarah smiled and hugged back.

Shortly after that, Maggie and Drew arrived flushed from the cold and excited to tell everyone that Jimmy was recuperating very well. "He is enjoying the video games that George and Sean sent over."

She and Drew also wanted at this time to *thank* everyone for all their efforts the night that Jimmy got lost. They would never be able to thank them enough for all the time in the cold they spent looking for him and the prayers that they shared to find their son.

"This is a Thanksgiving we will never forget," Maggie said with tears in her eyes.

Drew put his arm tenderly around his wife and said, "I would also like to add how grateful I am for all the love and special care you give to my beautiful wife and my children while I'm away. It's one less thing for me not to have to worry about overseas. I know that they are truly taken care of and protected here at home with such wonderful friends and neighbors. A husband/father just can't ask for more. So thank you all from the bottom of my heart, and what you all do here for our servicemen and women, well it really is amazing. Thank you, and happy Thanksgiving."

When Maggie realized that the tone was getting a bit too serious, she said, "Hey, it's Thanksgiving. We've got about thirty very hungry servicemen and women coming in about a half an hour. Isn't there anything we should be doing?" At that, hugs were given all around. Tommy walked in from the kitchen and asked if he could be a part of the hugging party. They all looked at him and swallowed him in one giant hug.

"Okay, okay, that's enough already. Happy Thanksgiving to you too," he said as he smiled at all of them gratefully.

———————— ⌒ ————————

Flynn came in from outside and asked everyone to join him in the foyer. As everyone came in and formed a small circle, they all looked at each other and gave a concerned look toward Flynn. He just smiled, and folding his hands together, he looked at each individual. Then he said with sincerity, "My friends, I cannot explain to you the gratitude that I'm feeling in my heart right now. This is, well, I can't even remember how many years we've been doing this. And each year, I feel more overjoyed than the first. My only regret is that my lovely angel, my wife, isn't still here to see that her idea so many years ago has blossomed into what it is today. Ms. Beam and Ginger had tears in their eyes and were dabbing them with Kleenex. Kate was blinking a lot as if willing her tears to stop.

The men were all alternately looking from their shoes to Flynn. Maggie didn't even try to hide her emotion and was closest to Flynn and was patting him gently on the back as he continued, "Well, I just want to say thank you. If it wasn't for you and all the folks that contributed to our feast, well, this just wouldn't be possible. You all are my friends old and new alike, and for that, I really can't ask for more, Happy Thanksgiving, everyone. Let's be sure to give these men and women who serve our country a Thanksgiving that they will really remember. Don't forget they're away from their families, and this is real tough for them. Let's be like family to them, make them happy and give them a meal to be thankful for.

Man your posts I think I see Pat bringing the first bus up the drive. Andy should be following right behind." Everyone eagerly scattered to their assigned areas leaving Flynn to open the door preparing to welcome their guests.

As Josh was heading into the kitchen, Drew caught up with him and asked if he could have a word with him. Josh smiled at him and said sure. They walked together back to the kitchen, and Drew took a deep breath and said, "It seems I owe you a huge thank you." Josh turned and with a questioningly look and, "Asked Why?"

"Well, my beautiful wife told me that if it hadn't been for you, our son might have died from hypothermia."

"I'm still a little confused," Josh said looking directly at Drew.

"You know the outerwear you bought my family."

"Oh that, that was nothing. We made a deal, and I was happy to help out. I'm sure it's difficult to live on a serviceman's salary and to be away so much. It makes life with a family a bit difficult. I'm just glad to be able to meet you and to see you back with your family. They miss you a great deal."

"Yeah, well, I miss them too. I just wanted to thank you and to let you know that we will pay you back. You don't have to worry about that."

"I have no doubt about the payback, Drew. I have all the faith in the world that you'll pay me back." They shook hands as they finished their conversation. Drew stopped short and looked at their hands and looked at Josh questioningly. Josh quickly defused the situation by smiling and giving a shrug of his shoulders. "My dad says it's a gift. Strange I know, but it's the best explanation I have at the moment."

Drew stepped back shook out his hand and said to himself as he walked away, *That's some gift.*

Flynn went outside to retrieve the turkey. Tommy, Maggie, and Drew met their guests at the front door. Ms. Beam took their coats. George and Ginger led them to their seats in the living room. Kate and Sean stood at the table waiting to help anyone with their dinners. Mac took drink orders. Josh was in the kitchen ready to fill and refill plates, platters, and bowls that would be coming in from the dining room empty. Each person there had a job and all were prepared to do it exceptionally well.

As everyone got their food and they were ready to eat, Flynn stood in front of the fire place and asked for everyone's attention.

All eyes were on Flynn. "Usually at this time I say a little prayer here and ask God to grace us and to give Thanks but this year I'm going to start a new tradition. This year I want to ask someone new to give the invocation. Josh, would you please come up and say a blessing before our meal?"

Josh was surprised and delighted at the same time. The rest of the group was also quite surprised, they new that Josh was spiritual. He did say prayers and blessings a lot, even when he wasn't asked. But this, this was special. Sean really thought it was strange, but he figured he'd just ask Flynn about it later. George and Ginger were thrilled and coaxed him up to the front. Josh got to the front and tapped Flynn on the shoulder and turned to the group and smiled. Josh raised his head and hands as everyone else bowed theirs.

Father, he began, Thank you so much for this special gathering of friends and the bountiful gifts of food and drink that sit before us. We thank you for all those whose generosity is shown by the abundance of this bounty that sits before us. We are so grateful for the sacrifices that these men and women make for us every day to keep us safe. We ask that you continue to keep watch over them and their families as they continue their vigil in honor of our safety and the promises made to keep our country free and independent. We also thank you dear Father for the gifts of our loved ones close by, those far away, and those who have gone before us. Amen, and happy Thanksgiving, everyone.

Everyone repeated a rousing amen, and the chatter of conversation began as well as the sound of clanging dishes.

The worker bees, as Flynn called them, all went to their stations. George, Ginger, and Mac went around to the tables refilling coffee, tea, and water for the guests. Kate, Maggie, and Tommy helped serve in the dining area. Ms. Beam washed dishes and filled the dish washer as dishes came in empty. Flynn walked around and visited with the guests. Josh and Drew continued to refill platters and bowls on the dining table as needed. Sarah had left earlier to be with her husband back at their home next door.

Soon all the guests had had their fill of pie, cake, cookies, and coffee and tea that were served for dessert.

At this time, all the helpers joined the guests in the living room. Flynn sat down and played some Christmas Carols on the piano, and everyone joined in for a good old fashioned sing-a-long. At eight o'clock, the busses pulled into the driveway and signaled to everyone that it was time for the men and women to head back to the base. Ms. Beam, Tommy, Ginger, and George helped with the coats. Flynn, Maggie, and Josh made sure that all the leftovers were given to the guests for them to finish up at the base. Drew, Sean, and Mac went into the kitchen area and brought out all the supplies and books that had been collected from the community and churches. Andy and Pat helped put them into the back of the busses. When the busses were all loaded up with people and supplies, everyone stood on the porch waving good-bye until the busses had disappeared down the road.

Chapter 19

Thanksgiving Reward

Back inside, the men got busy taking the chairs and tables down and putting the living room back in order. The women got busy pulling assorted food out of the oven that they had kept warm for themselves and bringing them out to the table in the dining room. There they set up another beautiful but smaller Thanksgiving dinner. All this time, Flynn had had another smaller turkey cooking on the grill. He went outside just then and brought it in. Once everything was set up, the living room was back to normal, the fireplace was stoked and burning brightly, and all the dishes from the guests were put away, Maggie and Drew said their good-byes. Everyone from the boarding house, Mac, Kate, and Tommy, sat down at the newly set dining table. This time, Flynn started with a bowed head.

Dear Father, we thank you for the lovely day, lovely friends, and lovely food. For these and all your gifts we are eternally grateful, Amen. And happy Thanksgiving"

"Amen, let's eat! Yeah!" said Tommy

"I'm starved."

"Me too," agreed George. "All agreed that today had been a great success. And as Josh looked around the table at all of his new friends—Sean, Ms. Beam, Kate, her husband Mac, George, Ginger, Tommy, and, of course, Flynn—he thought with a full heart,

Yes, the world is in trouble. That is true. Yet if what I just witnessed in the past few days is just a sampling of what is happening all over the world, then I know that my Father's creations are still doing his work to give faith and hope to those struggling…with even just a fraction of faith still visible, I know that my purpose here will not be in vain. With all the new friends I have made at Flynn's Boarding House and in the little community of Munising, Michigan, life will be full of challenges that I will look forward to them with open arms and an open heart. Josh

Let's Chat!

It's at this time that I would like to mention that the community activities in this story are true community projects. The Community Harvest Project has been done for years in our community. Each year, the Crystal Lake Jaycees and Chamber of Commerce has put this project together, and Thanksgiving morning for many people in our community starts out with a cup of coffee and sorting hundreds of pounds of food. The overall feeling is fantastic. The Share-A-Christmas Project is also a real project that the Crystal Lake Jaycees do every year. This program has been a great help to families in our community as well. Collecting for the US Vet is one that personally I have not been a part of. However, I did have a nephew in Afghanistan (shout out to Ryan), and I do know that these items mentioned in the book along with phone cards are easily obtainable and useful to our men and women overseas. Having a soldier over for Thanksgiving dinner is easy. Contact your local base or recruiting office to find the soldiers.